Danny stopped lau though she'd given going away next week. We'd have the whole apartment to ourselves." He gave Alex a meaningful look.

She shivered. "I thought you wanted to wait. You said you didn't think either of us was really ready. You said we should think about it."

"I have thought about it," Danny said. "Haven't you?"

She smiled shakily. "It's only when I think about it that I get scared. Like what I was saying before. If we just did it, it would be a lot easier."

He reached across the seat and took her hand. "Jean's leaving on Tuesday. I'm driving her to the airport. What if I picked you up on my way back? You could say we were going to the movies or something."

She nibbled at the ragged edge of her thumbnail. "It would have to be an early show. They don't like me to stay out late on weeknights." Alex giggled nervously. "Something X-rated."

Danny squeezed her hand. "Okay?"

"Okay," she agreed.

Other books in the SENIORS series – ask your bookseller for the titles you have missed:

WINNER ALL THE WAY
by Eileen Goudge

BANTAM BOOKS
TORONTO · NEW YORK · LONDON · SYDNEY · AUCKLAND

WINNER ALL THE WAY
A Bantam/Corgi Book 1985
UK edition published 1986

All rights reserved.
Copyright © 1984 by Eileen Goudge and Cloverdale Press Inc.
This book may not be reproduced in whole or in part, by
mimeograph or any other means, without permission.
For information address: Bantam Books, Inc.
61–63 Uxbridge Road, Ealing, London W5 5SA

ISBN 0-553-17259-X

Printed and bound in Great Britain by
Cox & Wyman Ltd., Reading

To Al Zuckerman, who makes it all come together . . . even when he's not looking over my shoulder.

With acknowledgement to Aaron and Jonah Zuckerman for sharing their diving experiences.

Chapter One

Alex was scared.

She always got scared just before a dive, but she would've died before admitting it to anyone. Especially her parents, who were watching her now.

She stood poised on the diving board, her stomach clenched as she stared down at the polished turquoise surface below. She flexed her knees slightly, forcing her body to relax. She had so many goose bumps she felt as if her skin had shrunk and was suddenly too tight for her body. She breathed in deeply through her nose, inhaling the damp chlorine smell.

It would be the first meet in which she'd ever attempted a combination dive this difficult—a backward somersault with two and a half twists. Sure, she'd pulled it off plenty of times in practice, but practice was different from a meet. This was the real thing, the A.A.U. sectionals, with a crowd of people watching.

Coach Reeves eagle-eyeing her every move. But most of all, her parents and Noodle *counting* on her . . .

She wished that her best friends—Kit, Elaine and Lori—could be here. But even though it was Saturday, none of them had been able to get away, especially since the sectionals were being held all the way over in Santa Clara. Kit had to work at the pizza parlor; Lori was baby-sitting; and Elaine was one of the bridesmaids at her cousin's wedding.

Oh well, if she won they would all celebrate tomorrow. And if she lost, they would be there to console her. That was how it was with them—they shared everything: the ups as well as the downs.

Out of the corner of her eye, Alex caught sight of Danny standing off to one side of the bleachers, behind the row of judges in their white suits. He was wearing his blue striped racing trunks, with a towel draped loosely over his tanned shoulders. His hair looked darker than its usual sun-streaked blond because it was wet. His eyes were the same clear, aquamarine shade of blue as the water. Calmly, he looked up at her and smiled. Alex felt the warmth of his smile wrap around her.

She tried to smile back, but her lips were frozen in place. Danny never got as nervous as she did, but then he didn't seem to care as much about winning as she did. He was a good diver—better than she in some ways—but he seldom attempted more than he thought he could safely pull off. Danny never would have shot for two and a half twists after only four weeks of practice, for instance. Too risky. It was better to score high in a less difficult dive, he always said.

She knew the message behind Danny's smile: *play it safe*.

But Alex never played it safe. She couldn't live with herself if she didn't push her mind and body to the limit. Taking a shot at winning was worth it . . . even if she failed in the attempt.

Three more points would put her overall score higher than anyone else's. Even a two-point-eight would tie her with Virginia Kirk, who had beat her out in last year's sectionals and was currently the reigning Junior State champ. She *had* to go for it. Second best just wasn't good enough.

Alex took another deep breath. The wind shifted and she was caught in a cool current of air that lifted the hair off the back of her neck and kicked up little flutters across the pool's surface. *Now*, she told herself.

Her heart racing, she sprinted the last few feet, leaping up and coming down hard and loose on the end of the board. Then she was in midair, soaring up and out the way she had so many times in practice, feeling all the tension

9

go out of her body like a released spring.

As always, this was the moment when her fear slid away like a bad dream, and the only thing she was aware of was the kaleidoscope of spinning sky and water as her body somersaulted through the air.

From board to water measured exactly three meters—roughly ten feet. But Alex wasn't thinking about that distance now. She measured it by instinct, sensing the precise point at which she must come out of the twist so that she would hit the water cleanly. Too many times she'd misjudged it and the dive was spoiled by a late, sloppy entrance that created far too big a splash.

Alex felt her body split the surface, clean as a knife. Underwater, she instinctively rolled into the tuck that would keep her from going too far and hitting her head against the bottom.

She kicked her way up with short, powerful strokes, breaking through in a small explosion of droplets to greet the applause that rained down on her from the bleachers.

She'd done it! A perfect dive! Every nerve and muscle tingled with her triumph. She wasn't surprised when the judges held up their scorecards—there wasn't one lower than a two-point-six. Her overall score was two-point-eight. Not perfect, but certainly good enough to tie her for first. Maybe even good enough for the state championship next month . . .

A pair of muscular brown arms reached down and hoisted her up as she was scrambling out of the pool. Alex looked up into Danny's grinning face. Before she had a chance to catch her breath, he scooped her into his arms, even though she was dripping wet.

"Wow, that was some dive. You were great! I wish I had a videotape of it so you could see for yourself."

Alex gave a breathless little laugh. "I'm glad you don't. I'd probably criticize it to pieces. You know how I am."

"Yeah, I sure do." A small frown flitted across Danny's features, then his sunny grin broke through again. Arm in arm, they strolled over to where their team was clustered.

Coach Reeves congratulated her with his usual bone-crushing handshake. "Nice timing, Alex," was all he said, but she could see how proud he was by the way his massive chest was pushed out, stretching the pocket on his polo shirt.

"I probably could've shaved another quarter of a second off that last turn," she said, going back over the dive in her mind. She accepted the towel and warm-up jacket Coach Reeves handed her. "It wasn't exactly perfect."

"We have plenty of time to work on it before the championship," he said. "Don't be too hard on yourself, Alex." He grinned. "Remember, that's *my* job."

Two more divers went after Alex, then the judges announced the final scores. As she'd expected, Alex was tied for first in her division. Danny had placed sixth in his, but he didn't seem too unhappy about it.

"I'm just not like you that way," he said with a shrug as they headed back to the locker rooms to change. "The way I feel is, it's great if I win, but it's okay if I don't. You're different, Alex. You *have* to win or nothing else counts. I guess that's the attitude it takes to be a champ, though."

"What's the *point* unless you care enough to want to win?" she countered.

It was an old argument between them, going back to when they'd first started dating—a year ago, when they were both juniors. Alex smiled to herself, remembering how they'd met. She'd been just as determined to win then, only the prize she'd been after was Danny himself.

They were in a lifesaving class together and had been assigned as partners in a test drill. Danny had been serious about that class— he'd wanted to get his credentials so he could get a summer job lifeguarding at the beach—so serious, in fact, that he hadn't seemed to notice that she was crazy about him. Alex had had to practically force him into kissing her by pretending she needed to practice mouth-to-mouth resuscitation.

They'd been together ever since. She loved Danny, and she knew he loved her, but it hadn't all been easy, even though they were a lot alike—on the surface, that is. They both loved to do outdoors stuff, for instance. In addition to swimming and diving, they spent a lot of time just riding around on their bikes. On the weekends when the weather was nice, they sometimes hiked up into the hills around Glenwood with a picnic lunch. There were lots of little creeks and waterfalls up in the woods where no one lived, so they could take off their clothes and play around in the water, or just stretch out in the sun. Once, seeing him sprawled on a sandbar, all gold and tawny and spattered with leaf-shadows, she teased him about being a reincarnated mountain lion. He'd growled and flipped her onto her back and . . .

They'd come so close that time. But she'd held back at the last minute. Something always stopped her. Maybe it was knowing that, underneath, they were very different people. Maybe she was afraid, deep down, that it couldn't last. Going all the way would just complicate everything, wouldn't it?

Danny must have felt the same way, because

the one time she'd weakened and decided "Why not?" *he* was the one who had held back.

Even though Alex loved Danny, she was a little bothered by his take-it-or-leave-it attitude toward competing. Winning was so important to her. She just couldn't understand how anyone with as much talent as Danny had could feel differently. Why bother at all unless you aimed for the top?

For the moment, though, Alex forgot her annoyance as she spotted her parents moving through the crowd that had spilled down from the bleachers. They never had too much trouble on that score, she thought—crowds had a way of parting for them like the Red Sea.

Her father was beaming. He looked very tall and important, like some kind of dignitary in his spotless cream-colored sport jacket. His black hair and golden-hued skin made a striking contrast to his light-colored clothing. Alex was amused by the fact that a lot of people didn't realize he was Japanese when they first met him, until they found out his name was Dr. Enomoto. Though she had to admit that her father had probably gotten most of his height from his mother, who was only part Japanese, the way Alex was.

Her own mother was a mixture of a lot of things, mostly Irish. She had brownish-blond hair and eyes the dusky-green color of mint leaves. Alex didn't think that either she or her brother, Jimmy, looked very much like their mother. They had inherited most of their looks from their father. Both she and Jimmy had dark hair and dark almond-shaped eyes, although Alex's olive-brown complexion had more to do with the time she spent outdoors than her Japanese heritage.

Alex didn't consider herself to be all that hung up on her looks, anyway. Oh, sure, if a fairy godmother came along and gave her a choice, she would have asked for a nose that didn't look as if it belonged on Benji, and she probably would've added a few inches to her neck while she was at it. But basically, she thought she looked okay. Not fabulous, like her friend Lori, or sexy like Kit, or brilliant like Elaine—but certainly okay.

Susan Enomoto caught up with Alex first, wrapping her arms around her. Alex felt her mother's pearls digging into her chest. She smelled the way she always did—like those little sachets you're supposed to tuck into the back of your underwear drawer (something Alex refused to do).

"Alex, I am so *proud* of you!" Her mother pulled back with a little laugh. "Not surprised, mind you, just very, very proud."

Over her mother's shoulder, Alex could see Danny's face. He was smiling, with one eyebrow cocked. He mouthed the words, *I'll see you later,* before sauntering off.

Then her father was hugging her, too. "Hi, Champ. You were sensational. Another performance like that at the championships and you'll wind up on the Olympic team before you know it."

Alex's stomach did its own double flip at the thought. What if she didn't make it . . . what then?

But she refused to consider that possibility. She had to make it—she just *had* to.

"Where's Noodle?" she asked. She wanted to share this moment with her brother more than anyone else.

Susan made a small fluttering motion with her hands. "All these people . . . he didn't want to make a fuss with the chair. He's over there, where we were sitting." She pointed back toward the bleachers.

Alex could see her brother, parked in his wheelchair at the far end of the bleachers. He looked very small from this distance, much younger than fifteen. The sun shining on his glasses had turned them into little orange suns.

"I'll be right back," she told her mother.

She padded back through the drying puddles that lined the hot cement alongside the pool. When Noodle caught sight of her, he broke into a wide grin. She sank down on the bench beside him, feeling the grooves through her nylon swimsuit where the wood had been

16

warped by hundreds of wet behinds.

"Cinch," he said. "I knew you could do it."

"*I* didn't," she confessed easily, leaning back and squinting into the sun, her elbows resting on the bench behind her. Noodle was the one person with whom she could be totally herself—nervous jitters and all.

"Yeah, well, that's how it works. Don't you see? If you *knew* you could do it, you wouldn't have tried so hard."

Smart. Noodle was so smart, Alex thought for the hundredth time. That's how he got his nickname. When they were both younger and one of them did well in school, their father would always say, "That's using your noodle." Only he ended up saying it a lot more to Jimmy, because he was so much smarter. Alex liked to think it was God's way of making up for the way Noodle had been born—by giving him twice the brain.

"I was so scared I thought I was going to throw up," she said.

"That's how I felt before my first big match," Noodle agreed. "Like the only thing standing between me and my breakfast was that chessboard staring me in the face."

She looked over at him and grinned. His hair stood up in uneven black spikes, the way it always did after he'd just gotten a haircut. Because he was so thin, his head looked slightly too large for his body, but she hardly ever

17

noticed those things anymore. Noodle was . . . well, *Noodle*. She could even make herself forget about *it* for short periods of time. Until he got sick again. *It* was the thing he'd been born with: cystic fibrosis, or CF, as the people who had it and their families called it.

"But you won," she recalled. "Didn't that make it all worthwhile?"

"Depends on how you look at it. Sure, I guess so." He shivered, drawing his thin arms across his chest.

"Cold?" Alex hadn't noticed it herself, even though she was wearing a wet swimsuit. She slipped off the warm-up jacket that was draped over her shoulders. "Here, put this on."

"I'm okay," he growled impatiently, but he put the jacket on anyway.

"Remember the last cold you caught," she reminded him. "You were in the hospital three weeks that time."

He laughed—a quick, dry laugh. "Yeah, good old St. Theresa's. I woke up and there was this priest standing over me. I remember thinking, *Hey, you can't write me off, I'm not even Catholic*."

Alex couldn't help laughing. It wasn't funny, but she'd found that a lot of the time you had to laugh in order to keep from crying.

She touched the back of his hand, resting against the arm of the wheelchair—lightly, so she wouldn't have to feel the ridges of bone his

18

flesh barely covered. The breeze ruffled her hair, which was almost dry already; she kept it short for that very reason.

"Aunt Charlotte sent you white chrysanthemums and Mom cried and made the nurses take them away. She said they reminded her too much of funerals," Alex recalled.

He smiled crookedly. "I don't remember that part. But it sounds like something Mom would say. She doesn't like to think about me dying."

"Who said anything about dying?" Alex was getting that old panicky feeling inside her chest again. "Anyway, you're too stubborn to die."

Noodle didn't say anything. He just kept staring out at the pool. Now Alex felt the cold, too. She shivered. She wanted to fill up the silence with words, but she sensed it was probably better not to. Instead, she gave him a quick hug and walked back over to her parents and told them to go on ahead without her—she was riding home with Danny.

"You know what our problem is? We think too much," Alex sighed later that afternoon as she snuggled close to Danny in the front seat of his Chevy pickup.

"About what?" he asked, playing with the string tie on her peasant blouse.

"About everything. School. Life. Us. We spend so much energy asking ourselves *why* we want to do something that half the time we don't end up doing it."

Mostly, she was thinking about her and Danny, and all the time they spent *talking* about things they never did. Like sex, for instance. Sometimes, she wondered why they didn't just *do* it without asking a lot of questions first. Life was so short. Who knew what their lives would be like tomorrow? For people like Noodle there was no tomorrow; there was only today, this very minute.

The other day she'd read an article in the paper about a girl her age, seventeen, who had died in a car crash, and she remembered thinking, *That girl could have been me.* Then she thought about all the dreams and maybe-someday-I'll-do-it promises she would have left behind, and it had made her sad.

Alex leaned her head back against Danny's shoulder and stared out at the ocean, which was the greenish color of old copper under a streaky orange sky. They had driven over to Half Moon Bay, about twenty minutes from Glenwood, and were parked on a low cliff at the end of a bumpy dirt road. They'd been to this place many times; Alex liked it because it was private and not too easy to get to, so there were rarely any people around.

She'd always wondered why it should be that way—that the harder a place was to get to, the fewer the people who went there. She thought

it should be the other way around. Since se-
cluded spots were usually the best places,
people should *want* to go out of their way. But
maybe that was just she. The more difficult
something looked, the more determined she
was to do it.

Danny kissed her lightly on the forehead.
"Come on, let's go for a walk before it gets dark.
That's one thing we don't have to think about
first."

The cliff was steep and mostly made up of
loose, slippery shale, but Alex managed to
scramble down by grabbing ahold of the vine-
like ice plant that dangled from every crack.
Danny was right behind her. When they were
almost at the bottom, he let loose a wild Tarzan
yell and swung down the rest of the way. He
brushed against her, making her lose her bal-
ance. Together, they toppled onto the beach
below in a heap of tangled limbs.

"Danneee!" she screeched, then started to
giggle.

Laughing, they rolled on the sand while she
pretended to punch him and he tried to pin her
arms to her sides. When she ran out of breath,
she stopped wrestling and lay quietly in his
arms.

"God, I'm covered with sand," she gasped. "I
think I even have some up my nose." She shook
her head, but that only sent more sand flying
up around her.

21

He grinned. "I like you this way. It goes with your personality. Gritty. Anyway, isn't that where pearls come from?"

In the fading light, Danny's eyes looked more gray than blue. The wind blowing in from the ocean parted his hair on one side, pushing it up into a peak.

Gently, he brushed the sand from her face with his fingertips. He bent close and kissed her, his mouth warm and sweet. Under the thin canvas of his Windbreaker, she could feel his heart beating very fast.

Alex wound her arms around his neck, pushing her fingers up into his hair. She wasn't even aware of the sand anymore. All she could feel was the warmth from his kisses spreading through her.

They went on kissing for a while—Alex couldn't tell how long. Minutes? Hours? Kissing Danny was like traveling to another country, and every time she went there she got lost. Lately, it had been getting harder and harder for her to find her way back . . .

Danny slid his hand up underneath her blouse. Cool air tickled her bare stomach. Suddenly, all her clothes felt too tight. Her jeans itched at the waistband where sand had gotten in. She wanted to take them off. She wanted to feel Danny's warm skin against her.

She smiled sleepily up at him. She didn't have to say anything. It was their secret signal.

22

They both wriggled out of their jeans. Alex wasn't worried about being seen. The beach was completely deserted, the nearest house a pinprick of light above a distant, neighboring cliff.

Sand sifted across her stomach, down her legs, as she shifted so that their bodies lay close again. They were naked except for their underwear. The air in her lungs felt hot and dry in contrast to the chill air that rippled across her bare skin. A mixture of panic and excitement pushed its way up into her throat.

His hand moved up her leg. They'd gone this far before, but never all the way.

She wanted to. They both did. In one way. But in other ways, they were afraid. It wasn't just she. She knew Danny felt the same way. They'd talked about it.

But somehow, at this moment, all their reasons and arguments seemed as distant and unthreatening as that pinprick of light on the far cliff. She felt different. Natural and free. They weren't groping for each other in the front seat of his car, with the steering wheel getting in the way. Or sneaking up to his room while his parents were gone, having to scramble for their clothes every time the stairs creaked.

Besides, they loved each other, didn't they? Danny would never hurt her or force her if it started to seem wrong.

"Danny," she murmured. "Let's take off all our clothes."

Something icy and wet licked her toes. She yelped and jerked upright.

Danny groaned. "The tide. Shoot, we forgot about the tide," he said as a pale finger of foam stretched up the beach.

They pulled on their clothes as fast as they could, but even so, her ankles and the cuffs of her jeans ended up getting wet. When they were back in the pickup, Danny started the engine and turned on the heater.

They looked at each other and began laughing.

"It's not funny," she said, and they laughed even harder. "Even when we don't think about it, look what happens. Remember that night over at your sister's? We should have then. It would have been nice. Does she still have that waterbed?"

Danny stopped laughing and just smiled, as if she'd given him an idea. "She's going away again next week. Her company is always sending her places. I'm supposed to water her plants."

He gave Alex a meaningful look.

With the stale air from the heater drifting up around her, she shivered. "I thought you wanted to wait. You said you didn't think either of us was really ready. You said we should think about it."

24

"I have thought about it," he said. "Haven't you?"

She smiled shakily. "It's only when I think about it that I get scared. Like what I was saying before. If we just *did* it, it would be a lot easier."

"Sure, but what if we had done it just now? Neither of us was, uh . . ." His tanned cheeks reddened slightly. "What I mean is, some things you have to sort of prepare for."

"Aren't you . . ." She found she couldn't say it either, even though she usually had no trouble talking about these kinds of things. Well, with her friends, anyway.

"I could get some," Danny put in quickly. "On Monday, at Rexall's . . ." His color deepened. "Unless, that is, you . . ."

She shook her head. "I've always been too scared. Sometimes it's not so great having a father who's a doctor. What if I went to someone for birth control and he turned out to be a friend of my father's? No, I think it would be better if you . . . well, you know, took care of it. Do you mind?"

He reached across the seat and took her hand. "I don't mind. But are you sure? Do you want to go ahead with this?"

Alex took a deep, shaky breath. "Sure I'm sure. But I guess we'd better decide when. You know, just so we can get ourselves prepared."

"Jean's leaving on Tuesday. I'm driving her

25

to the airport. What if I picked you up on my way back? You could say we were going to the movies or something."

She nibbled at the ragged edge of her thumbnail. "It would have to be an early show. They don't like me to stay out late on week-nights." She giggled nervously. "Something X-rated."

Danny squeezed her hand. "Okay?"

"Okay," she agreed.

Tuesday, she thought. *In three more days, I won't be a virgin anymore. Can I really go through with this? How can I live until Tues-day?*

Chapter Two

"Don't get me wrong—I want to, I really do. It's just . . ." Alex stopped in the midst of lifting a Hefty bag full of empty soda cans and looked up at Elaine. "It seems so strange, planning it like this. Like going out and buying a car . . . or getting married."

She tossed the bag into the back of Danny's truck, which she'd borrowed for the day. It landed with a hollow crash against the other bags that were already piled there, which they were taking over to the recycling center. Alex and her friends had volunteered to spend Sunday afternoon gathering up the bags of cans the senior class had collected for their Pic-Up-A-Can Drive to raise money for the Senior Picnic next month. They were at head cheerleader Roseanne Parker's mock colonial house in Glenwood Acres. The last stop.

Elaine groaned. "Please, don't remind me. If getting married is anything like being a bridesmaid, I plan on being single for the rest of my life. Do you know what it's like standing around in the hot sun for two hours getting your picture taken? I might not have minded so much if they'd at least let me pick my own dress. But I had to wear this dress my cousin bought for me. It was this awful grayish pink—you know, the color bubble gum gets after you've chewed it a while." She stooped to retrieve a can that had rolled out of one of the bags. "On the other hand, if I ever do get married, I suppose the wedding night will make up for a lot of it. Though I'll probably never know what *that's* like, at the rate Carl and I are going."

She sighed wistfully, pushing her glasses back into place as she straightened. There was a smudge of dirt on one cheek, which Alex had the urge to wipe away. On the rare occasion when something was awry with Elaine's appearance, it looked as out of place as a mustache on the Mona Lisa.

Not only was Elaine the smartest person Alex had ever known, she was also the neatest. Everything about her—from her straight, shoulder-length brown hair to her sensible Weejun loafers—was always perfectly in place. Today she was wearing a plaid shirt and jeans, but they weren't just *ordinary* jeans. Compared to her own faded Levis and baggy sweatshirt, Elaine looked as if she'd walked straight off a page of the L.L. Bean catalogue.

But even though Elaine's neatness exasperated her sometimes, Alex knew that she was as interesting and zany on the inside as she was preppie looking on the outside. Those big tortoise-rim glasses might hide the fun-loving twinkle in her brown eyes, but that only made her humor all the more deadly. Like that time in the eighth grade when Elaine and Kit had hooked an old bra they found in the locker room on that plaster bust of Beethoven Mrs. Horton kept in the music room. Kit got the blame then, not Elaine. In fact, no one could believe Elaine had had anything to do with it, even after she confessed—no one except Alex, that is. Even now, all one of them had to do was hum a few bars of Beethoven's Fifth and they'd all crack up in hysterics.

Right now, she could see that Elaine had her own problems where her boyfriend, Carl, was concerned. Even though they were the opposite of her own, she sympathized.

"Has he kissed you yet?" Alex asked.

Elaine sighed again. "I'm not sure."

"How can you not be sure?"

"It was hard to tell. It happened so quickly. I think he was aiming for my mouth but it landed mostly on my cheek. Or maybe it was the other way around—he was aiming for my cheek, and it landed on my mouth. We were both sort of embarrassed afterwards." She finished loading the last bag onto the truck. "Last night was our third date. If something doesn't happen pretty soon, I may have to resort to drastic measures."

Alex giggled. "You mean like seducing him?" Somehow, she just couldn't imagine Elaine doing a sexy siren number on Carl. Elaine probably couldn't either.

Elaine blushed. "Uh . . . not exactly. I don't think I could ever go *that* far."

"Maybe you should draw him a diagram. You know, like Mrs. Sanderson used to in Special Assembly," Alex teased, remembering how embarrassed they used to get when the school nurse gave the sixth grade girls those what-it's-like-to-be-a-woman lectures.

Elaine gasped. "Oh, Alex, you're *awful*!" She was grinning, but her face was redder than ever. "I wouldn't crack any jokes like that around Danny if I were you. It might make him nervous under the, uh, circumstances."

Alex clutched her stomach. "Whenever I think about it, I get this funny feeling, like I'm on a roller coaster. I don't see how I can last until Tuesday."

She got into the front seat of the truck, and Elaine slid in beside her. They were on their way over to the recycling center now, where Kit and Lori would meet them with the cans they'd collected.

"I guess it's hard, no matter which end

you're on," Elaine commiserated. "Are you scared you won't like it—is that it?"

Alex thought about it for a minute, then said, "I think I'm more afraid that I will. What if we like it so much that's all we'll ever want to do? What if it gets in the way of my diving? Winning the championship means *everything* to me."

"I don't think it's that way with Kit and Justin," Elaine said. "They do other things."

"That's true," Alex agreed. "I guess what bothers me is, I just don't know how it'll turn out. It's like that second or two just before a dive when you're wondering if you're going to pull it off okay, or end up blowing it completely."

"What about something in-between?" Elaine said, with her usual level-headedness. "You know, maybe it won't be all that sensational, but maybe it won't be so terrible, either."

Alex started the truck up and shot out of the driveway. As she was barreling down the street, she noticed out of the corner of her eye that Elaine was clutching the door handle. Remembering how nervous it made Elaine when she drove fast, she slowed down.

"It's the in-betweens I don't know what to do with," Alex sighed. "I really hate losing, it makes me mad. But at least when I'm mad I can go out and kick a garbage can or some-

31

thing. What do you do with an in-between?"

They were driving through the main part of Glenwood now, along a street shaded by oak trees and lined with quaint, touristy shops. A small modern-looking shopping center lay just beyond where the local people shopped. The recycling center was down one of the narrow side streets in a white barnlike building.

Alex caught sight of Kit's orange VW as she was pulling into the parking lot. Kit was perched on the hood. She jumped off when she saw them, bounding over.

Alex suppressed a smile at how totally unaware Kit seemed to be of the stares she was attracting from the two teen-age boys stacking lumber nearby. She was wearing a pair of tight cut-offs and a skimpy midriff top. She looked like an advertisement for a sexy movie.

Not that she could've hidden much, even in baggy clothes, Alex thought. Kit had the kind of figure that didn't just enter a room. The only way Alex could describe it was that Kit had a way of *exploding* on boys wherever she went.

Alex had mixed feelings about the commotion Kit's sexiness usually created. She didn't think it was right for girls to get noticed just because of their bodies. She didn't envy Kit—she liked her own body pretty much the way it was—but it sometimes bothered her when boys stared at her friend, as if there were nothing more to Kit than a dynamite figure.

Once, as a joke, she'd given Kit a T-shirt that said on the front, "All this and brains, too." What it should also have said was that Kit was kind and generous as well. Though she tended to be scattered when it came to getting places on time, or turning her homework in when she was supposed to, you could always rely on Kit for the things that really counted. Like lending an extra hand without having to be asked, or just *being* there when you needed a friend. Kit was probably the only person Alex had ever known who would actually lend the shirt off her back if someone asked—although Alex had to admit that most of Kit's shirts would be too revealing for anyone else.

"Hi!" Kit greeted them, pushing her tousled butterscotch-blond hair out of her eyes. "I guess I got here kind of early, but there are only so many cans you can squish into a VW."

While Elaine went inside to find someone to weigh their cans, Kit helped Alex unload the truck.

"Where's Lori?" Alex asked. "I thought she was with you."

"She was," Kit said. She stopped to tighten the laces on her sneakers which prompted a low whistle from one of the boys as she bent over. Up close, Alex could see that Kit was blushing, even though she pretended not to notice the attention she was getting. "I don't know what happened—it was the funniest thing. One minute she was fine, then all of a sudden she just took off. I think it had something to do with seeing Perry Kingston."

"Who's Perry Kingston?"

"Oh, you probably don't know him. He's new. He just transferred to Glenwood last week. He's in our Psych class and sits next to Lori. The crazy part is, he's really adorable and seems to like her, but she's been avoiding him like the plague. I don't understand it.

"Well, Lori's awfully shy. Or maybe she thinks he's stuck up."

"No. I don't think Perry is the conceited type. Listen to this. He comes from the same school Lori used to go to before she moved. I wonder if he knows her? Remember, she said it wasn't a very big school."

Alex shrugged. "You know how secretive Lori can be."

Kit looked puzzled. "I could understand it if he were creepy or something. But he's not. He's really cute." She shot Alex a mischievous grin. "Don't tell Justin I said so, though. He gets jealous sometimes."

"I can't imagine why," Alex said, keeping her expression deadpan. "You still didn't tell me what scared Lori off just now."

"I don't know. Perry showed up a few minutes after we did. He had a lot of empty boxes—from unpacking all his stuff from moving, I guess. Anyway, the minute Lori saw him,

34

she got all jumpy and said she had to go. Just like that."

Alex knew that Lori didn't have far to go. Her house was less than a fifteen-minute walk away. She wondered if maybe they should stop over at Lori's house on the way home. That way, if something was bothering her, they might be able to help.

Kit was obviously thinking the same thing. "Let's go to Lori's after this," she suggested. "Maybe if we all gang up on her at once, she'll have to break down and tell us what's wrong."

Twenty minutes later, they were on their way. Alex was the first to arrive at Lori's. Elaine had decided to ride with Kit, whom she felt safer driving with, since Kit rarely went faster than the speed limit.

Lori cracked open the front door cautiously in response to Alex's knock, almost—Alex couldn't help thinking—as if she'd half-expected to find Jack the Ripper standing on her doorstep.

"Oh, it's you." She breathed a sigh of relief, opening the door wider to let Alex in.

In the living room, Alex sank down on the big flowered couch by the window. Everything about Lori's house was flowery. Outside, flowers covered practically every square inch of the backyard. Inside, it was the same. The carpet was green with pink cabbage roses, and even the drapes had some sort of flowery design. Fresh-cut gladiolas filled a large vase that sat on the fireplace mantel.

In some ways, Lori reminded Alex of a flower, too. A rose, perhaps. That was probably a corny comparison, but it was true. Lori was that pretty. She had a sort of fresh, pinkish glow about her—like those models you saw in shampoo commercials, and her long blond hair looked as though the sun were shining on it even when she was indoors. Her eyes were cornflower blue, even bluer than Kit's, and when she moved, she did it so quietly she almost seemed to float.

Lori did almost everything quietly. She usually didn't talk very much, except when she was with her friends, and even then it was in this soft, whispery voice. Alex realized she spoke this way because she wasn't very sure of herself, but she couldn't help thinking how ridiculous that was. If anyone ever had a reason to be conceited, it was Lori.

The fact that she wasn't stuck-up was one of the things Alex loved best about her. Because Lori was so sensitive about herself, she had learned to be extra careful about other people's feelings as well. If she ever did accidentally hurt someone—like the time she inadvertently led on Rusty Hughes, a boy Elaine liked—she usually wound up feeling more miserable than the person whose feelings she'd hurt.

"Want something to eat?" Lori asked. "I was just making myself some lunch."

"Sure," Alex said, suddenly realizing how hungry she was. "I'm starved. Better make enough for four, though. Kit and Elaine'll be here any minute."

She followed Lori into the kitchen to help her with the food. Lori got some salami and cheese from the refrigerator, while Alex unwrapped the loaf of bread she unearthed from the bread box. She was as familiar with all her friends' kitchens as she was with her own.

"You looked like you were afraid someone was going to attack you when you opened the door," Alex said as she spread mustard on a piece of bread. "Who were you expecting?"

"Uh, nobody." Lori let her long hair fall in front of her face, a little trick she had when she wanted to hide the fact that she was blushing. "I always get a little nervous when Mom's not home. Once, our next-door neighbor got robbed—in broad daylight. Nobody was home at the time, but I keep wondering what would've happened if someone *had* been."

"I know what I'd do," Alex said, with more bravado than she knew she probably would have felt in that situation. "I'd get the can of Mace my mother keeps in her closet and blast them with it."

Lori giggled. "You *would*. I'd be too scared. I'd probably do something really heroic—like

37

faint."

Alex sawed off a piece of salami to chew on while she made the sandwiches. "There's this girl in my Chemistry class, Anita Bergstrom. Something like that happened to her. She was walking her dog one night and this guy tried to grab her, so she told him her dog was trained to attack on command, and he *believed* her!"

"What's funny about that?"

"Come on—a *chihuahua*?"

They were both giggling helplessly when Kit and Elaine arrived. Suddenly, the tiny kitchen was in an uproar as they all swapped stories, each one more outrageous than the next. Alex cut up the rest of the salami, while Kit sliced the cheese and Elaine got out the pickles and lettuce. Lori finished making the salad.

"Is that *all* you're eating?" Elaine asked Lori when they all sat down at the kitchen table. The only thing on Lori's plate was a tiny portion of salad.

"I'm on a diet," she said.

Kit groaned. "Not *again*."

Alex couldn't see why Lori was always dieting, either. She wasn't the least bit overweight, even though she seemed to have a deathly fear of getting fat. In a pair of white shorts and daffodil-yellow T-shirt, Lori looked slim and gorgeous, as usual.

Of course Lori wouldn't say *why* she had such a hang-up about being fat. It was just one of the things she didn't like to talk about. Like her father, for instance. Alex knew he was dead, but that was all, except that it had happened before Lori moved to Glenwood, which was last year. She never talked about him otherwise.

Lori wouldn't talk about Perry, either, when Alex finally brought up the subject. She just repeated the same thing she'd told Kit—that she didn't know him, and he must have mistaken her for someone else. When Kit and Elaine pressed her, Lori just clammed up, the way she always did when a subject made her uncomfortable.

Alex chalked it up to another one of Lori's mysteries, and decided it would be better to drop all questions for the time being. If and when Lori wanted to confide in someone, she knew who her friends were.

When they were finished eating, they all went outside to sit on the patio in back. It was hot but they were partially shaded by the arbor that a client of Lori's mother had built. Mrs. Woodhouse was a lawyer who was always taking on cases for people who couldn't afford to pay her, so often they gave her something like this in return. Alex would never forget the time one of her clients, a baker, donated a sheet cake the size of a parade float for a slumber party Lori had. They'd eaten so much they'd made themselves sick.

Alex loved Lori's backyard. It was full of plants and flowers, most of them hanging in tubs from the latticed redwood arbor—begonias, azaleas, and something Lori called baby's tears. Lori was responsible for most of it; gardening was her favorite hobby. It was a talent Alex really admired, but wouldn't have had the patience for herself.

Alex filled Lori and Kit in on her problem concerning Danny. Not that she considered it a real problem, exactly. It was just something that happened to be very much on her mind at the moment.

"I'm beginning to wish we hadn't waited so long," she said. "We've probably built it into something it can never live up to. Besides, I can't get rid of this picture I have of Danny walking into Rexall's and asking for a dozen you-know-whats. It seems sort of cold and calculated, even though I know he'll probably be horribly embarrassed. *I* would be."

Not many things embarrassed her, but there *was* a limit.

Kit had slipped on a pair of oversize sunglasses that made her look more like a movie star than ever as she lay sprawled on the chaise longue, one leg dangling over the side.

"I know what you mean," she said. "Justin told me what it was like the first time he did it. The man behind the counter asked him what kind he wanted—plain or assorted colors."

40

"Colors?" Elaine choked, turning pretty red herself. "They come in *colors*?"

Kit nodded, her lips pressed together to keep from laughing. "Mmm."

"What kind did he get?" Alex asked, filled with curiosity.

"He didn't get anything. I guess he was too flustered. He told the man he'd have to think about it, and walked out."

Lori shrank down in her lawn chair. "God, how embarrassing! I would hate the thought of some stranger knowing something like that about me. It seems so, well, personal. Like having someone know what kind of underwear you've got on."

Alex giggled. "You sound like my mother. She's always telling me I shouldn't wear underwear with holes because you never know if you're going to get into an accident and then someone might see it. Personally, I couldn't care less. I just like to be comfortable. Anyway, if I got into an accident I don't think any doctor would be looking to see if I had holes in my underwear. I know my father wouldn't."

"You're father's a dermatologist," Elaine pointed out logically. "That doesn't count."

"What about Danny?" Kit asked, sitting up and sliding her sunglasses down her nose to peer at Alex. "Are you planning on wearing anything, uh, special for Tuesday?"

Alex made a face, which was really just a

cover-up for the panic attack she felt coming on whenever the word *Tuesday* was mentioned.

"If you mean something sexy like a see-through nightgown or a black bra, the answer is no. Absolutely not. I don't want to make this into any more of a production than I can help. As it is, I'm starting to wonder if this planning-it-all-out business was such a good idea."

"I don't think it makes much difference either way," Kit said, flopping back with a sigh. "It's never what you'd expect. At least I know it wasn't for me."

"What *was* it like?" Lori asked in her whispery voice, her cheeks pinker than usual.

She'd admitted before that she was curious about sex, but hadn't had much experience. In spite of the fact that boys were always chasing her, she hadn't gone any farther than kissing. Poor Lori, Alex thought, she would probably die from embarrassment if a boy's hand ever got higher than her knee.

"Nice," Kit confessed with a dreamy smile. "At least that's the way I felt afterwards. While it was happening, I guess I was sort of in shock. I hardly knew what I was feeling."

Kit usually didn't like discussing the intimate side of her relationship with Justin, Alex knew. It was a pretty private subject with her. Most of what she told them was general stuff;

she never went into detail.

Alex sighed, picking at a begonia blossom that had fluttered down into her lap. "I suppose I am more worried about how I'm going to feel afterwards. Danny and I . . . well, we love each other, but sometimes . . . I just wonder."

"About what?" Elaine asked.

Alex wasn't sure she knew herself—it was just a feeling she'd had lately. If she were the superstitious type, she would've called it a premonition.

"I'm not sure," she said softly. "Maybe it's crazy, but I've been sort of nervous about us these past few weeks. I think it has something to do with the championship. Danny says I'm putting too much emphasis on diving, but I don't think he's putting *enough*. He says if I didn't practice so much, I'd have more time for other things. Like being with him. So . . . I can't help wondering if maybe part of the reason he wants us to do this thing is because he thinks it'll bring us closer together."

"What do you think will happen if you *don't*?" Elaine asked.

Alex shook her head. "I don't know. I honestly don't know sometimes."

Abruptly, Lori scrambled to her feet. "Come on, let's run through the sprinkler. I'm getting hot."

Elaine looked down at her neatly pressed shirt and jeans. "I don't have my bathing suit."

Kit jumped up, too. "So what? We never worried about bathing suits when we were kids. Let's!"

Alex was the first to peel off her clothes as Lori set up the sprinkler on the small strip of grass that bordered the patio. She wasn't worried about being seen. Lori's backyard fence was solid and nearly six feet high. Kit took off all her clothes, but the more modest Elaine and Lori kept their underwear on.

Shrieking as she raced naked through the icy spray, Alex forgot her worries and just gave in to being silly and carefree. She had the odd feeling she was hoarding something precious that wasn't going to last much longer.

Chapter Three

"That wasn't fair. You cheated," Alex grumbled, scooping her chess pieces into a pile. "You lost on purpose that time."

Noodle grinned as he leaned back, hooking one arm over the back of his chair. "Unfair is when you cheat to win," he pointed out with maddening logic. "Besides, I didn't lose on purpose. Much as I hate to admit it, you're getting pretty good. Maybe one of these days you'll be as good as I am."

"Ha!" she grunted.

She didn't believe it for a minute. Besides, there was another reason she would never be as good as Noodle, one she didn't like to mention. Diving, as well as her other activities, kept her on the run so much of the time she hardly ever had the opportunity to sit still for a game of chess. She couldn't help feeling a little guilty about this, even though she knew it was nobody's fault, except maybe God's, that Noodle had to sit still all the time.

She and her brother had fallen into the habit of playing a game or two every other Monday night. That was when Mom and Dad met with their CF support group, which was made up of a lot of other parents whose kids had cystic fibrosis. Though no one ever said anything out in the open, Alex knew she was expected to stay home with Noodle those nights. He would've resented anyone calling it "baby-sitting," but the truth was he couldn't be left alone—in case he got one of his attacks when he couldn't breathe.

Anyway, she didn't mind. It seemed there were never enough opportunities for them to be alone together these days. Someone was always hovering over Noodle—Mom or Dad, or Jan, his physical therapist. And when he was in the hospital it was the doctors and nurses. Noodle jokingly claimed he was used to being "public property," but Alex knew how hard it was for him. He hated being poked and prodded and having needles stuck in him all the time, even though he seldom complained.

"One more game," Noodle said, "This time I promise I'll skunk you."

Alex set up her pieces on the polished marble and alabaster chessboard Noodle had won as second prize in last year's Junior State chess championship.

"At least make it a fair fight," she said. "I

don't mind winning, as long as it's close."

"Famous last words," he scoffed. "I wasn't concentrating last time. Now you're really going to get it—both barrels."

It was a good game. Alex played sitting on the carpet in front of the coffee table, with her legs tucked up underneath her. As a matter of principle, she avoided the big white couch that was the centerpiece of the living room. She didn't like white couches, or anything else you had to worry about getting dirty while sitting on.

Mom, of course, hadn't taken that into consideration when she'd designed this room, and all the other rooms in the house. She was a fantastic designer and not just in graphics, either, which was her profession. But privately Alex felt she was just too much of a perfectionist sometimes. Undoubtedly she had this picture in her mind of the way a house *should* look—like something out of a fancy magazine. Only Alex had noticed that all those photographed rooms in magazines had one thing in common: there were never any kids in them to mess things up. She knew it wasn't that Mom didn't want kids around. Just the opposite— she was too protective sometimes, especially with Noodle. Maybe it was just that she liked having some things in her life the way she *wished* they could be, instead of how they really were.

Alex had already decided that when she grew up, she would live in the kind of house where you could throw wet towels down on the floor when you got out of the shower, where the carpet was a dark color instead of light beige, and the fireplace was something you could light big smoky fires in instead of stacking a few logs inside for decoration.

She had another fantasy about growing up, too, one she had never shared with anybody. This one was about Noodle. She fantasized that four years from now, while she was off winning Olympic gold medals, he'd be at college getting his degree in Physics. Someday, they might even share an apartment if neither of them was married. But even after they got married, they'd still be close. They would get together a lot. Noodle would teach her children how to play chess; she would teach his how to swim . . .

It was a good fantasy, even if it wasn't a very realistic one. Still, she clung to it, even though *realistically* she knew that most CF victims don't make it past eighteen or so. Noodle was different, she told herself. He was special. God wouldn't end his life so soon.

Her thoughts were interrupted when Noodle crowed, "Checkmate!" He moved in against her last pawn with his queen.

It was close, even though Alex realized she'd only had half her mind on the game. Maybe

Noodle was right. Maybe she'd gotten better without even knowing it.

He was grinning at her, his dark eyes flickering with mischief behind the thick lenses he wore.

She stuck her tongue out at him playfully. "I would've beat you that time except . . ."

"The sun was in your eyes, right?"

When she was younger, her father had taught her to play tennis. Even then she'd hated losing, so she always made up an excuse—like the sun being in her eyes. Noodle teased her about it so much it got to be a joke. Whenever she botched anything, even if it was only a homework assignment, he would say, "Don't tell me—the sun was in your eyes, right?"

"You dope," she said, lightly tossing one of the pillows off the couch at him. He ducked, and it ended up knocking over a Chinese vase filled with silk flowers that was on the piano. She laughed. "*That* time the sun was in my eyes."

After she'd finished straightening up the flowers, she went into the kitchen to get something to eat. Noodle steered his wheelchair over the plastic runners that had been laid down over the carpet. The runners made it easier for him to move his chair, but they also kept the carpet from getting too dirty.

Alex got out the half-finished quart of

fudge-ripple ice cream that was in the freezer. Noodle wasn't supposed to have ice cream, so he helped himself to some applesauce instead.

She watched him take two bites and push his dish aside.

"Not hungry?" she asked.

He shrugged, getting that faraway look again. Softly, he said, "I talked to my counselor today. Mr. McKinney says I have the credits to graduate next year if I want. He's sure I can get into Stanford."

When Alex told people her brother was in a special school, they naturally assumed it was because of his handicap. He'd been in a wheel-chair since the age of ten because he couldn't get enough circulation in his feet, on account of his illness. But the school Noodle went to was "special" only because it was for very bright kids.

"That's great!" Alex said.

But Noodle only nodded, his expression solemn. "I guess it is."

"But it's what you always wanted, isn't it? You haven't changed your mind?"

"No, I haven't changed my mind. It's just . . . sometimes it seems so pointless. Chances are I won't graduate. Even then . . ." he shrugged.

There was no self-pity in his voice, only a kind of awful resignation. It was that matter-of-factness that Alex found even more unen-

50

durable than the rare times he broke down and got really upset. She swallowed hard against the lump that was forming in her throat. Noodle was just being honest with her. She knew she was the only one in the family he could really talk to about his fears and the hopelessness that overwhelmed him at times. They had always understood each other better than either of their parents did. The only thing was, she never knew what to say in return, and this inability to say something comforting and reassuring made her feel as if she were somehow letting him down.

She stared into her bowl, at the ice cream that was melting into a soupy blob. Her eyes swam with tears.

"You have to be all right," she said. "You just *have* to, okay?" She looked up at him, forcing a smile that felt more like a grimace. "You want to see me win the gold medal, don't you?"

Noodle's grin popped back into place. "Wouldn't miss it for the world. But, hey, are you sure they let wimps compete?"

"I'll pretend I didn't hear that."

Alex went back to eating her ice cream. She relaxed, feeling her tears subside. Everything was going to be okay . . .

Maybe if she told herself that enough times, she could make herself believe it.

In the middle of the night, she was jerked

awake by a familiar sound—harsh, desperate choking noises coming from the next room, Noodle's room. Light spilled into the hallway from her parents' room. She heard the frantic rustle of her mother's nightgown, the squeak of her father's slippers.

"Help me! I can't breathe!" Noodle gasped in a thin, strangled voice.

Alex lay rigid beneath the covers, listening to those sounds that made up such a large part of her life. Several times a week, Noodle woke up in the middle of the night, unable to breathe, too panicked to find the oxygen that was kept by his bed. Mom or Dad, sometimes both, would get up and help him, then sit with him until he could get back to sleep.

She waited, unable to relax, until she could hear the slow, faint hiss of the respirator. Then she slipped out of bed, shivering as her feet touched the cold floor. Pulling on her old terrycloth bathrobe, she crept down the hall to her brother's room.

Mom was sitting on the edge of the bed. The light from the hallway fanned across her face, showing all the worry lines she managed to hide with makeup during the day. Her short, brownish-blond hair, which was normally bouncy and fluffed up, straggled about her shoulders.

Noodle lay flat under the covers, his skeletal body barely making a mound in them. His face was in shadow, but she caught the gleam of plastic tubing that pumped oxygen from the respirator through his nose. The only movement was the labored up-and-down motion of his chest.

"Mom?" she whispered. "I'll sit with him, okay?"

Her mother shook her head, answering softly, "I'm all right, honey. Get back to sleep. You have school tomorrow."

"I want to. Please?"

Her mother looked at her, then rose with a tired nod and went out of the room.

Alex sank down on the bed. Noodle was clearly too exhausted to speak, but he managed a tired smile for her benefit. When they were little kids, she used to sneak into his room after their parents had gone to bed. She would scrunch down under the covers with him and tell him stories she made up on the spot to help him get his mind off how bad he was feeling. Dumb little stories that didn't make any sense, but Noodle loved them. He would ask her to repeat certain ones, but they never came out the same the second time, which was probably one of the reasons he was so crazy about them. He liked stopping her halfway through and saying, "I thought you said the princess's name was Poppy, not Violet," or "Didn't the alligator eat him up the last time?"

Alex touched his hand, which felt cold. CF had stunted his fingers, giving them a clubbed look he was ashamed of. She curled her own fingers about his, as if she could somehow pass her warmth into him.

The words came to her before she fully realized she was saying them. "You see, once there was this alligator named, uh, Winston. Yeah, that was it—Winston. He wasn't much to look at, but he was very smart. He lived in the moat outside the castle of a princess named Violet, who was beautiful but very dumb . . ."

Chapter Four

"No, Alex!" Coach Reeves bellowed across the water. "You came out of the pike too late. Do it again—this time nice and clean."

Alex swam to the edge of the pool. She was exhausted. Her arms and legs felt like iron weights, and there was a funny buzzing in her ears. She'd gotten up at five o'clock in order to be at school by six. She was going in early every morning, since she'd begun seriously training for the championship.

She hauled herself up and over the edge, her skin contracting into goose bumps as the cold air hit her. She trotted back to the board, following the trail of wet footprints left by her previous dives. The chrome rungs of the ladder felt like ice against the soles of her bare feet.

Three rungs from the top, she paused and looked down. Coach Reeves was standing directly below. She could see the top of his head where his hair lay in thin wisps across his bald spot. The pool area was empty except for one other person: a husky blond man sitting in the bleachers, watching her every move. He wore a light-blue Windbreaker that matched his eyes. Alex didn't know who he was or what he was doing here. She guessed he was a friend of the coach.

Then she was at the top, and suddenly she was all alone, where the blue sky and water below belonged only to her. She lifted her arms and felt the morning breeze wash over her like an invisible river. She forgot how tired she was. The heaviness drained out of her arms and legs. Her head stopped buzzing.

She dove, sailing out in an arc, arms spread-eagled for one marvelous instant before she dipped into the pike. Touch the toes. Arms up again. The water seemed to reach up and pluck her out of the air. It wrapped around her, feeling warmer than it really was.

She floated lazily to the surface, breaking for air only when she ran out of breath.

"Nice, Alex." Coach Reeves helped her over the edge. "I think we can call it a morning. Before you go, though, there's someone I'd like you to meet." He gestured at the lone figure in the bleachers.

The man got up and ambled over. He stuck out a large, square hand. "John Nylander." Before she could open her mouth, he said, "I know. You're Alex Enomoto. I've been hearing a lot about you."

Coach Reeves was beaming as he slung an arm about John Nylander's broad shoulders. "John coaches Olympic contenders," he explained. "He used to be on the Olympic team himself. Won the bronze back in '72."

It turned out that the two men were old high school buddies. They'd both been on the school swim team, but only John had made it into the Olympics. Alex could hardly believe they were the same age. John looked much younger than thirty-five. He reminded her a little of Robert Redford.

"Grant told me you had Olympic potential," he said. "Frankly, I had my doubts. Good is one thing. Great's another. You have to be great to make it on the team, and there aren't many of those. But," he nodded in the direction of the diving board, "seeing is believing."

Alex couldn't believe what she was hearing. An Olympic coach thought she was great! Her ears started ringing again, but this time it was like the aftereffect of deafening applause. Her heart was pumping so wildly she was sure he could see it through her yellow nylon racing suit.

She was only dimly aware of it when John continued, "I'd like to work with you, Alex. Of course I'll want to see how you come out at the championship first. But don't worry." He grinned at Coach Reeves. "You're in good hands now."

Her coach tossed her a towel. "Go on, hit the showers. You're not there yet, so don't get a swelled head." But he was grinning as he said it.

Alex left the two men to exchange words as she walked—no, floated—into the locker room. She hurriedly stripped off her suit and stepped into the shower. There was no one else in sight. As the hot water sluiced down and a cloud of steam boiled up around her, Alex let go of the wild-Indian whoop that had been building inside her.

This is crazy, she thought. I get up at the crack of dawn after being up half the night with Noodle. I kill myself doing laps, then I dive myself numb. And I've never felt more wonderful in my whole life.

Crazy, she repeated to herself. But she was grinning so hard her face felt as if it would split in two.

By noon, she was a wreck.

"What if I blow it?" she sounded off to her friends. "What if I don't make the grade?"

Elaine reached across the lunch table to touch her arm. "You won't blow it, but even if you did . . . well, you'll have other chances."

Alex shook her head. "John Nylander won't be interested in me if I don't place at the championship. This is it. A chance like this only comes along once in a lifetime."

"I know what you mean," Lori said, nibbling on a carrot stick. "Did I tell you who's coming to give a talk on Career Day? I just found out myself—Shandra Britton."

"Who's Shandra Britton?" Kit asked.

Lori gave her one of those you've-got-to-be-kidding looks. "She was only one of the highest-paid fashion models in the business! Her picture was on the cover of practically every magazine published. She doesn't model anymore, but she has her own agency and goes around the country recruiting girls for it. And she's coming *here*, to Glenwood, in a couple of months. I can hardly believe it!"

Alex knew that Lori wanted to be a fashion model someday. It was her secret dream, although so far it hadn't gone past the dreaming stage. Lori was too shy to take any action. Also, she didn't think she was pretty enough. Ha!

"That's great!" Alex told her, hoping Lori would get the chance to fulfill her dream, too. Maybe if Shandra Britton told her what a fantastic model she'd make, Lori would finally believe it.

Lori smiled at her. "What I meant before was—I know how you feel about being nervous. Every time I think about meeting Shandra, my stomach just drops right out from under me."

They were eating outdoors at one of the picnic tables on the cafeteria patio. It was too nice a day to be inside, they'd all agreed. Lori was the only one brown-bagging it, though. She was still on her diet, Alex observed, watching her crack open a hard-boiled egg after she'd finished her carrot stick.

"That's not the only thing I'm nervous about," Alex confided, lowering her voice. "Tonight's the night. Danny's picking me up after he drops his sister off at the airport."

Kit had seemed distracted about something, but she pulled herself together to ask, "How does Danny feel? I mean, have you talked to him about it?"

"Not really." Alex picked at a loose splinter on the table. "I don't think either of us wants to admit we might be making a mistake."

"You can always change your mind," Elaine said. "There's no law that says you have to go through with it if you don't want to."

"I want to . . . at least, I think I do . . . I don't know . . ."

"Elaine's right—maybe you should wait until you're sure," Lori put in.

"What if I'm never sure?"

"Whatever you do, just don't force it," Kit advised. "That time I almost did it with Rich Garrison up at his cabin—well, deep down inside, I knew it wasn't right. But I kept telling myself it would get better. I don't know why I thought it would, I just did."

"Rich was a real creep," Alex said. "It could never be like that with Danny."

"No, of course not," Kit said. "It's just . . . even with the *right* person sometimes the timing can be wrong. There are still times with Justin when"—she hesitated, blushing—"well, when one of us wants to and the other one doesn't. It doesn't mean we don't love each other."

Kit wore a thoughtful expression as she gazed out over the quad where a small crowd had formed to watch the cheerleaders practicing a routine. Some kids were sitting cross-legged under the big eucalyptus tree that had the initials of half the couples in school carved into its trunk.

Alex had noticed that Kit seemed less bouncy than usual these past couple of days. Were Kit and Justin having problems? She hoped not. They seemed so perfect for each other. But then, that's what a lot of people said about her and Danny. It was never the same looking in from the outside as it was the other way around, from the inside looking out.

Well, at least Kit didn't *look* miserable, she thought. In a shocking pink halter-top and a denim mini-skirt that showed off her shapely tanned legs, she looked ready to take the world by storm. Well, at least the male population of it, Alex reflected in amusement.

"I read a letter in Dear Abby once," Lori said.

"It was really sad. This girl said she wished she and her boyfriend *had* planned it all out first, then maybe she wouldn't have gotten pregnant."

Kit rose abruptly, mumbling something about getting a book from her locker. Even though she had her head lowered, Alex caught the glint of tears in her eyes. Lori must have noticed it, too, because she wore a stricken expression, obviously afraid she'd said something wrong.

"Wait. I'll come with you!" she called, dashing after Kit.

Alex turned to Elaine. "What's wrong with Kit?" she asked, truly concerned.

Elaine looked a little worried, too. "I don't know. Her mother's got a new boyfriend. You know how Kit wishes she would settle down. Maybe it has something to do with that."

"Maybe." Alex nibbled on an oatmeal cookie. That could have had something to do with it, but Kit hadn't really gotten upset until Lori brought up the subject of being pregnant. She wondered if . . .

Her own stomach knotted at the thought of Kit being pregnant. Poor Kit! She hoped it wasn't true.

The prospect of tonight loomed in her mind. Suddenly, everything seemed so complicated. When she had fallen in love with Danny, she hadn't thought about anything more than kissing him. Would it go on getting more and more complicated? Would she end up worrying about the things Kit probably worried about—like getting pregnant? And what would she feel like if they ever broke up? How would she feel about not being a virgin if she went out with other guys? Would someone else *expect* her to go all the way? Would she expect to herself?

Then again, the prospect of *not* going all the way with Danny seemed awful, too, in its own way. The feeling of always being on the edge, about to fall over . . .

She looked over at Elaine—solid, dependable Elaine. Her friend even looked the part in a sensible herringbone skirt and plain white blouse, her brown hair clipped neatly back with a tortoiseshell barrette that matched her glasses. Alex couldn't imagine Elaine ever facing a situation like this. But if she ever did, she would probably do the sensible thing—whatever that was.

"How's Carl?" Alex asked, longing to escape her own predicament.

Elaine sighed, a smile playing at her lips. "He came over last night. We were up in my room studying. I was supposed to learn the constellations, and Carl said the best way to do that is just to look up at the sky. So I turned off the lights, and we both lay down on the bed so we could look up at the skylight. . . ."

"Mmm. Sounds romantic."

"It was. I really thought he was going to kiss me that time. He even took my glasses off. Then he put his hand against my cheek, and kind of turned my head so that I was facing him. Like this." She demonstrated with her own hand. "Maybe it was my imagination, but it seemed like he was breathing funny, too. You know, like he'd been running or something . . ." she trailed off.

"Then what happened?" Alex pressed, eager to hear how it came out.

"Then my little sister walked in," she finished flatly, dropping her chin onto her hands, supported by her elbows. "She wanted to know what eight plus four equaled . . . and why we were going to bed without our pajamas on." She smiled ruefully. "When you live in a big family, nothing, absolutely *nothing* can surprise you after a while."

Alex giggled. "I guess I'm lucky that way, though I always wondered what it would be like, having a sister or two. Of course, my parents couldn't . . . well, after Noodle was born, they didn't want to take the risk of . . . of another child having what he has."

"You're lucky," Elaine said. "You could have been born with it, too."

"I know." That thought had occurred to her, too. More than a few times, as a matter of fact. She felt guilty about it even though it didn't make any sense to feel guilty about something you had absolutely no choice in.

Choices. For everything you got, you had to give something up, didn't you? Like the flip side of her being born healthy was that Noodle had to be born sick. Alex knew her parents would never have taken that chance with a second child if *she* were the one who'd been born with CF. There was no way for a couple to know if they were carriers of that bad gene until they had a kid like Noodle. Every time she leaped off that diving board, free as a bird, she felt it—maybe just for a flicker of an instant, but it was there—the knowledge that Noodle would never soar like this. . . .

Maybe going all the way with Danny would be sort of like that—giving up something in order to get something. What she didn't know exactly was what she'd be getting . . . or what she'd be giving up.

Elaine must have sensed her mood, for she reached over and squeezed Alex's hand reassuringly.

"Don't worry, Alex. It'll all work out somehow. Remember, you're a winner."

Am I? Alex asked herself. Sometimes she wondered.

Chapter Five

The last time Alex had been in Danny's sister's apartment, it had felt warm and cozy, with its jungle of hanging plants and the bright handwoven Mexican blankets tacked up on the walls. But tonight, standing here with Danny, it seemed so alien. She felt like an astronaut about to set foot on the moon.

She walked over to the nearest chair, a big, overstuffed monstrosity Jean said she'd bought at a flea market, and plopped down. She decided the best thing to do was to act as if this were a perfectly normal visit. Nothing to get excited about. Still, she wished her heart would stop beating so wildly.

"Don't you think . . ." Danny began, his own nervousness showing in the way his voice cracked, rising a few octaves. He cleared his throat. "I mean, wouldn't it be better if we took off our coats?"

Alex looked down at her old navy pea jacket,

surprised to see she was still wearing it. "Uh, yeah," she said, her own voice sticking in her throat. "It is a little hot in here." Hot? Oh my God, would he think she was eager, straining at the bit to go through with it?

She took off her coat. She was glad she hadn't bothered to dress up. She was more comfortable this way—in jeans and a T-shirt—than if she'd worn some slinky, sexy number. At least this way she could be herself, not some Brooke Shields clone.

Danny had taken his jacket off, too. He was looking around for a place to sit down. The trouble was, Jean's apartment was very tiny. The only place to sit down, other than her chair, was the waterbed that doubled as a couch.

Now he was looking at her again. "We could both sit on the bed if you want."

Because of all the hanging plants, the room seemed lit with a cool, greenish glow. Even Danny's eyes, which were normally the bluest of blue, looked a little green. Like her, he was wearing an old pair of cords, a T-shirt, and a pair of Adidas running shoes. He pushed his sun-streaked hair off his forehead with a quick, nervous gesture.

Alex stared at the bed, which all of a sudden seemed the size of a football field. It sprawled before her, looking as if it might swallow her up if she dared go near it.

"I'm thirsty," she announced, abruptly getting up and going into the kitchen. She found a glass in one of the cupboards and filled it with lukewarm water from the tap. She carried it back into the living room, sipping it slowly.

Danny was crouched in front of the stereo, sifting through his sister's record collection. He picked out a Carly Simon album and put it on. Carly's husky voice drifted from the speakers. She was singing "Anticipation." Alex groaned inwardly. A Hollywood director couldn't have planned the scene better.

"Jean only listens to soft music," he said, as if apologizing for the obviousness of his choice. "She says it's better for the plants. Do you believe all that stuff about plants being able to hear?"

"I don't think they actually hear things. It's something to do with vibrations."

"Yeah, that makes sense." He sat down on the edge of bed, which caused it to slosh from side to side.

Alex remained standing in the middle of the room, sipping her water even though she was no longer thirsty. *Were people subject to vibrations the same way plants were?* she wondered.

This is ridiculous, she told herself. *We're acting like we're on a blind date*. Everything felt stiff, and awkward. She didn't know what she should say next. She didn't even feel like herself. It was as if some stranger had come along and stepped into her body, and now that stranger was doing all the talking.

"Should we water the plants?" she asked.

"No, Jean said she watered them before she left. They'll be okay for a couple of more days."

She looked at him and smiled shakily. "I guess we're sort of avoiding the real reason for coming here, huh?"

Danny grinned. "Kinda seems that way, doesn't it? Look, Alex, we don't have to if you don't feel like it. I mean, you can still change your mind."

"Do you still want to go through with it?"

"Sure. If you do."

"It feels so funny."

"What?"

"Well, usually it kind of sneaks up on us. I'm used to that. It seems funny knowing in advance what's going to happen. It's like knowing ahead of time that you're going to fall off a cliff or something."

"I wouldn't exactly compare it to falling off a cliff."

"Okay. I didn't mean it had to be bad. I was only talking about the unexpected part." She looked at him hard. "Danny, were you telling me the truth when you said you hadn't done it before? I won't be mad if you have. I just want to know."

He got up and put his hands on her shoulders. Up close, his eyes were blue again, a deep drowning blue.

"I would never lie to you about something like that, Alex."

"I'm sorry. It was a stupid question."

"No, it wasn't. I understand how you feel. I would've told you if I had." He kissed her, softly, his lips tentative against hers, as if he were asking, *Okay? Are you ready now?*

She was trembling as she pulled back. "Did you . . . I mean, are you . . . ?"

He nodded. "It's okay. I took care of it."

She was silent for a minute, wondering what came next. Finally, she said, "I guess we should take off our clothes."

He smiled. "That might make it easier."

They stood there, looking at each other, neither of them making a move. Then they both erupted in uneasy laughter.

"I was waiting for you," she said.

"Ladies first," he teased. "Here, I'll help you." He peeled her T-shirt off inside out. Her head emerged in a crackle of static electricity.

She giggled. "It reminds me of when I was little and my mother used to undress me. It's okay, I can do the rest myself." She struggled out of her jeans, hopping around on one foot while she tried to yank the other leg free.

"It might help if you took your sneakers off first," he observed with a straight face, his eyes twinkling with amusement.

Alex was glad now that she had, at the last minute, thrown on the only pair of semi-fancy underwear she owned—a matched bra and panties set Kit had given her on her last birthday. They were a pretty pinkish-orange with darker paisley swirls. At least it was better than holey underwear.

When they were both naked except for their underwear, Danny said, "Why don't we lie down on the bed?"

"Okay."

She went over and lay down. Danny stretched out beside her. The bed rolled uneasily beneath them. For some reason, she felt cold, even though the room was warm. She couldn't stop shivering even after he pulled a blanket over them.

"Somehow, I never imagined making love on a waterbed the first time," she said.

"How did you imagine it?"

"I don't know. On a mountaintop maybe. Or in front of a fireplace with a storm blowing outside." She smiled. "Or on a beach."

"At least we don't have to worry about the tide coming in."

"Not unless this thing springs a leak. Are you sure it's safe?"

It was his turn to smile. "I guess we'll find out."

He stroked her under the blanket. She snuggled closer. She could feel the tension in his

71

body. They were both trembling. He rolled onto his side, facing her. The bed sank even lower beneath her. Then he was kissing her, while his hand moved lower under the blanket.

Oh my God, she thought, *it's really going to happen*. She felt dizzy, the way she always did before an important dive. Or was she already falling, spinning in midair, uncertain only of where and how she would land?

They stopped kissing to come up for air. She took a deep breath to steady herself, resting her head against his chest. She was glad Danny didn't have a hairy chest; she'd always hated hairy chests—they reminded her of animal pelts. She smoothed her hand across his stomach, feeling the hard bands of muscle underneath. With her ear pressed to his chest she could hear the powerful whooshing of his heart.

Now, he was struggling with the hooks on her bra. Her toes curled involuntarily as she felt the elastic give. Her own heart was beating so hard, she was sure something inside her would give, too. Abruptly, he stopped, pulling away slightly.

"What's wrong?" she whispered.

"Nothing." His voice was an agonized croak. He rolled onto his back. "Oh, damn. It's no use."

"Danny . . . *what*?"

"I . . . can't." He sounded as if he were in pain.

Suddenly, she understood. She'd heard about this happening with men sometimes. It had never seemed to be a problem with Danny before. She felt his embarrassment, but didn't know what to say. She was embarrassed, too.

"It's okay," she said, stroking his arm.

She felt his body tense. "This isn't the way I wanted it to be."

"I don't mind. Really." She couldn't decide whether it was true or not. Part of her was relieved, part of her disappointed.

It was obvious, though, that Danny felt awful. "I was pretty nervous," he said. "I'm sorry, Alex."

"You don't have to be sorry. I was nervous, too."

"Were you? I never know with you. You always seem so cool about everything."

Alex couldn't help being a little annoyed. She always got annoyed when he said that. Why did he go around assuming that about her? She got nervous, too, she just didn't show it as much.

"Do you want to get dressed?" she asked.

Danny nodded miserably. They got up, pulling their clothes on in silence. Danny didn't try to kiss her or put his arms around her. His expression was blank, almost stony. She knew it was only because he didn't want her to see how bad he was feeling.

In a rush of sympathy, she grabbed his hand as they were leaving. "Danny?" she said softly. "We can try again another time, can't we? Just because it didn't work out this time doesn't mean it won't the next."

He managed a smile, his expression softening. "I guess you're right. When we go camping next weekend, maybe we'll have a chance to sneak away from the others for a little while. Maybe, like you said, up on a mountaintop . . ."

Alex bit her lip. She'd forgotten all about the Sierra Club hike she and Danny were supposed to go on next weekend. It was an overnight trip, something they'd signed up for months ago. The plan was for their group to hike up into the mountains on Saturday, where they would camp out, then come back on Sunday.

She'd been concentrating so hard on her training, everything else had slipped into the background. Next weekend, like this one, she'd planned on devoting to diving practice. Saturday, John Nylander was coming to the pool to watch and offer her a few tips. There was no way in the world she could miss it if she wanted to do her very best at the championship. She would have to cancel the hiking trip.

"Danny . . . I won't be able to make the trip.

I have to practice."

He gave her a long, incredulous look. "Wait a minute, what is this? We had it all planned about the trip. You can't just back out at the last minute."

"I honestly forgot. I'm really sorry. It's all this pressure about the trials."

"Pressure?" He gave a bitter laugh. "The only pressure you're under is what you put on yourself. You never seem to have time for anything else these days. I stopped counting the dates you've canceled on account of diving practice. Is that all that's important to you, Alex—winning?"

She bristled. "Of course it isn't!"

He faced her in a squared-off position, his jaw stuck out at an angle. His blue eyes glittered with defiance.

"Prove it," he challenged. "Come with me next weekend."

Alex felt a surge of defiance. Why was he doing this to her? Didn't he know how important the championship was to her? That didn't mean he wasn't important, too. But there would be other camping trips, and this was her only shot at making the Olympic team. . . .

At the same time, she felt a certain, horrible inevitability about the whole thing. She'd seen this coming. There had been other hints along the way, smaller arguments—all of it leading up to this. True, it might not have come to a head this soon if things had worked out differently tonight, but it would have happened sooner or later.

"I can't," she said in a tight voice, fighting the tears that crowded near the surface. "Please try to understand, Danny. I just can't go."

"Yeah, I understand all right," he answered coldly. "I understand what's really important to you. And what isn't." He yanked the door open. "Come on, let's go. I've already taken up enough of your time. I'm sure you have better things to do."

They walked in silence out to his truck. Alex wanted to say something, anything that would make it okay, but she sensed that the rift was too big for words to fill. They were such different people . . . with such different goals. She still loved him, but was love always enough?

It wasn't until after he dropped her off in front of her house that she gave in to her tears. All her unhappiness and frustration came welling up in one gigantic, choking rush. Rather than face her parents like this—didn't they have enough to worry about with Noodle?—she sank down on the porch steps. Resting her forehead against her knees, she cried her eyes out, feeling as if she'd just lost something that was more important to her than she'd ever realized.

Chapter Six

School on Wednesday was a nightmare for Alex. Even before her first-period class, she knew it was going to be one of those hopeless days when everything goes wrong.

At practice, she managed to mess up on all but the simplest dives. She did so badly that Coach Reeves took her aside afterwards and asked her if she was feeling all right. Alex told him yes, she felt fine, even though she didn't—she was heartsick over what had happened with Danny. Also, to be truthful, she was angry, too. She thought Danny had behaved unreasonably, though she realized he'd been upset at the time and partly forgave him because of it. Still, she couldn't escape the fact that they would never see eye to eye about certain things. When it came to competitiveness, they were as different as night and day.

First period, she had PE. But the Phys. Ed. teacher, Miss Castle, announced that the badminton play-offs would be canceled today. Instead, they were having a special girls-only assembly. The guest speaker was Ms. Emily Leibowitz from Planned Parenthood. To Alex, the whole thing seemed like a conspiracy to remind her of last night's dismal experience.

Filing into the auditorium, she spotted Kit sitting in the second row. She hurried over, sliding into the empty folding chair beside hers.

"Do you know what this is all about?" Alex whispered.

"Some kind of lecture about birth control," Kit whispered back. She looked edgy. "The boys are getting it next period."

Alex thought of Danny, and groaned.

"I know what you mean," Kit said. "I'm not exactly wild about the idea, either." She sighed. "I think it has something to do with Monica Woollery."

Alex vaguely recalled the stories that had been circulating around the school a couple of months ago, at the time Monica dropped out of Glenwood High. She had been four months pregnant then. It was rumored that Pete Hansen was the father, but Pete said that was impossible. According to him, "They'd never taken a shower without a raincoat on," which was his way of saying they'd never Done It without a condom.

Ms. Emily Leibowitz turned out to be not

much older than Alex and her friends, or at least that was how she looked. She wore her frizzy reddish-brown hair pulled back in a ponytail and had no makeup on. She wasn't very pretty, but Alex thought she had an interesting face, which, to her, was more important.

The lecture lasted half an hour. Emily talked mostly about the tragedy of teen pregnancy, and how it was on the rise in high schools all over the country, in spite of all the forms of birth control that were available. Then she passed out pamphlets that described each method of birth control in detail.

"It might not apply to some of you right now," she said, "But I hope you'll read it anyway. It's important to know all the facts."

Afterwards, there was a short question-and-answer period. A number of girls raised their hands.

"This friend of mine thinks she might be pregnant," ventured Candace Jenkinson, a quiet girl who had been going steady with the same boy since her freshman year. She was sitting a couple seats down the row from them, so Alex could see how red her face was. "She doesn't want to tell her parents because she doesn't want them to find out that she's . . . well, she doesn't know what to do."

Emily kindly told her she should urge her friend to take advantage of Planned Parenthood's free pregnancy test. Then, if it turned out to be positive, she could talk to one of the counselors about what her options were. Right now, though, she said, the important thing was not to panic. A lot of pregnancy scares were false alarms.

Other hands shot up, but the bell rang before she could call on anyone else. She thanked everybody for coming, which Alex thought was a little silly since they didn't have much choice in the matter. All in all, though, Alex decided it had probably been very helpful to a lot of girls.

Alex was quiet as she and Kit walked to their lockers. She was thinking about Danny. Kit, too, appeared to be wrapped up in her own thoughts.

Kit was the first to break the silence. "Love is a pretty complicated thing, isn't it? I mean, just when you think you've got it all figured out, wham!—something happens to show you how crazy you were for ever believing it could be easy."

Alex saw she had tears in her eyes. Forgetting her own problems for the moment, she quickly steered Kit into the nearest bathroom.

"It's empty," she said after a quick check under the stalls. She faced Kit squarely. "So you can start by telling me what's wrong. I'm your friend, Kit. I *care*. Whatever it is, I want to help. And I'm not letting you out of here until you tell me what's bugging you." Lapsing into a phony German accent, she added, "You vill see, I haf my methods of making my prisoners confess." Laughter, she had long ago discovered, was her best strategy as far as dealing with her friends went.

Kit made a noise that was halfway between a giggle and a sob. Her shimmery blue eyes spilled over, the tears leaking slowly down her cheeks.

"That's not a bad idea, you know," she hiccuped. "If I could hide out in here, maybe my problem would be solved."

Alex ran cold water over a folded-up paper towel and handed it to Kit. "That bad?"

"Worse. Oh, Alex." Her voice caught. "I think I might be pregnant."

Kit's words hit her like a jolt, even though she'd been half-expecting them. She slipped an arm about Kit's shoulders. They stood facing each other in the big mascara-flecked mirror over the sinks. Alex felt as though they were watching a movie of themselves.

We could call ourselves *The Odd Couple II*, she mused. They were so different looking. Kit all golden and round in all the right places, looking positively adorable despite the fact that her makeup was all smudged under her eyes. With her usual eye-catching style, she wore an oversize pink sweatshirt over a purple striped mini-skirt. By contrast, Alex looked dark, all angles and edges, her hair a shiny mahogany-colored wedge next to Kit's sleepy blond tumble. Her own clothes reflected her streamlined style—jeans and a leotard top.

"How late are you?" she asked Kit.

"A week."

"That's not very long. I'm sure it's too soon to panic. Remember what Ms. Leibowitz said."

Kit's face puckered up with worry. "But I'm *never* late! Honestly, Alex, they could time the space shuttle lift-off by me. That's not all, either." She lowered her voice. "I got this book on, you know, symptoms." She whispered the word as if she were talking about some horrible contagious disease.

"Those kinds of books could scare anybody," Alex pointed out, trying to be reassuring. "I remember once when I was about ten or so, I had these red blotches on my arm. I looked up 'skin diseases' in my father's medical encyclopedia and ended up convinced I had leprosy."

Kit smiled in spite of herself. "What was wrong with you?"

"Poison ivy. I blew up like a balloon and spent a week in bed, but, boy, was I relieved. See what I mean? You can psych yourself into believing anything if you're in the right frame of mind."

Kit sniffed, blotting her eyes with the wet paper towel. "I guess you're right. I . . . I just can't help worrying, is all. If I got pregnant now, it would wreck everything."

Alex remembered Kit telling her once that she and Justin weren't always as careful as they should be about birth control. Alex wanted to say that she shouldn't be taking those kinds of chances, but she sensed that now wasn't the time for a lecture.

"Maybe you should go have that test," she suggested instead, "even though you're probably not pregnant. Then you can stop worrying about it."

"I'm scared," Kit confessed in a small voice. She leaned her head against Alex's shoulder. "What if I really am? At least this way I can tell myself maybe it's just my imagination."

"The trouble with hiding your head in the sand is that, even though you can't see it, the trouble out there keeps getting worse and worse." Alex sighed. "Like with Danny and me. I kept telling myself our differences didn't really matter. But I was just hiding from the truth."

Kit looked up with a concerned expression, her own worry apparently shelved for the moment.

"What happened with you and Danny last night?" she wanted to know. "Did you . . . ?"

Alex shook her head. She didn't want to go into any embarrassing details. Kit would understand, she knew.

"We had a fight," she said. She told Kit about

canceling out on the hiking trip, and how angry Danny had been. "He doesn't understand how important this championship is to me. Why can't he see?"

Kit was thoughtful for a minute, then said, "Maybe he does. Maybe he just doesn't like the idea of it being more important than he is."

Alex felt a surge of defiance. "What's so *wrong* with wanting to win. Lately, Danny's been acting like my ambition is some kind of weird addiction or something. He's always making me feel like I have to choose. Why should it be a matter of choice at all? Why can't *both* be important?"

Kit shrugged. "You're right . . . only it doesn't always work that way. I guess that's the difference between the way something *should* be, and the way it really is. Before my parents got divorced they were always fighting about that—about how my mom's career was taking up too much of her time. She said a woman's career should be just as important as a man's, and of course she was right, only—well, after my father moved out, she said something I'll never forget—she said that being right wasn't going to keep her warm in bed at night."

At least I don't have that to worry about, Alex thought. "I don't care," she flared stubbornly. "I love Danny, but that doesn't mean I have to give up everything else I love just because of him."

"Is that what he's asking you to do?"

"Not exactly. But he might as well be. If I couldn't compete . . ." she stopped. "Well, I guess it would be about the worst thing that could happen to me right now."

Kit hugged Alex. "No, it wouldn't. You'd still have Danny, and your family . . . and us. Besides, there are lots worse things. Like . . ." she added woefully ". . . getting pregnant."

Alex hugged her back. "Love *is* complicated," she said, recalling Kit's earlier statement. "Remember when we were thirteen and all we talked about was how neat it would be to get kissed?"

Kit's giggle backfired into a sad hiccup. "We used to practice on our pillows at slumber parties."

Alex stared at their reflection, searching for some reminder of the girls they'd been not so long ago. She remembered the Kit who'd worn braces and who'd actually stuffed her bra with Kleenex the summer of her thirteenth birthday. At the time, Alex herself had been even skinnier than Elaine, with long black braids that made her look like Pocahontas, and knees that were continually plastered with Band-Aids.

Alex felt a twinge of sadness—something she couldn't quite put her finger on. They'd been so eager to grow up; seventeen had seemed like such a glorious, magical age. And in a lot of ways it had turned out to be as exciting as they'd hoped. But still . . .

· "I wonder," she said, "if we'd known then what we were getting ourselves into, would we still have been so eager to grow up?"

Chapter Seven

"You're still a little loose on that tuck." John Nylander crouched down by the edge of the pool as she hauled herself out of the water. "Try to keep your knees together more. Remember, those judges are going to be shaving off points for every little mistake."

Alex tried the dive again, concentrating harder than ever. She wanted so badly to impress him! What if he decided he'd been mistaken to have thought she was so great before?

This time, though, John was smiling. His blue eyes crinkled up at the corners, as she swam back over to the edge.

"Hey, that's more like it, Alex! You're looking good. One more go at that last layout and we'll call it a day."

Alex had one foot on the ladder when she caught sight of a familiar figure watching her from the other side of the Cyclone fence that surrounded the pool area. Her heart lurched.

Danny! He was staring back at her, not smiling.

Alex walked back over to John. "Would you mind if we skipped this one? I see someone I have to talk to."

John glanced over at Danny, who was the only other person in sight. "Boyfriend?"

She nodded, swiping at a strand of wet hair that was stuck to her cheek. She hoped it was still true.

John clapped her on the shoulder. "Sure. Go on. You can make it up next time."

Alex walked slowly over to the fence. Her heart was pounding, and her throat was so dry there was a clicking sound in her ears when she swallowed. Danny often met her after practice when they weren't working out together. This Saturday, though, she hadn't expected him to show up. They'd been avoiding each other since Tuesday—a record-breaking cold war for them. In the past when they'd argued, they usually made up within hours. But Alex had a gut feeling that this was different. Although she'd missed him terribly, she'd dreaded this confrontation without really knowing why. Now, seeing the tightness in his face as she approached him, Alex knew why.

"Hi," she said, hooking her fingers through the smooth wire mesh of the fence. It seemed somehow symbolic to her, the fence, of the invisible barrier that lay between them. "I didn't think you were coming."

"I wasn't planning to," he said in an odd, stilted voice.

"I'm glad you did, anyhow."

"I only came by to see if you'd changed your mind about next weekend."

"Danny, I . . ." she bit her lip.

She wanted desperately to say something, anything, that would make it all right between them. These past few days without Danny, she'd felt so empty, even though she still believed she was doing the right thing. Feeling you were right about something didn't always make it easier, she'd discovered.

But the truth was, she hadn't changed her mind. Her diving was too important. Working out with John today had shown her how much she still had to learn. With the championship less than two weeks away, she'd have to work harder than ever. . . .

"I love you, but I have to do this," she finished awkwardly. "Maybe after the champ—"

The look in Danny's blue eyes cut her off. They were like chips of ice. He scooped a handful of sun-streaked hair off his forehead, and she saw that his hand was trembling slightly.

He shook his head. "Nothing's gonna change. You and I both know that. If you place at the championship it'll only get worse. Then it'll be the Nationals, and the next four years after that you won't be thinking about any-thing but the Olympics."

"That isn't true!" she argued. "You make it sound like . . . like I'm some kind of machine. You're not being fair!"

"Maybe I'm just being honest for a change. Maybe you don't even know it yourself, because this is the first time it's ever come down to making a choice. You think you can have it all, but you can't. No one can. The trouble with you, Alex, is you're looking up so much of the time, you don't see what's going on around you."

Alex felt bruised and shaken by his words—the way she felt when she fell out of a dive and landed wrong. She was angry, too. What right did Danny have to judge her? He didn't know what it was like having parents who expected you to be better than everyone else. Danny's parents were happy that he'd placed at all in the sectionals; they didn't care that it was only sixth. And Danny didn't know what it was like having a brother like Noodle either. If winning was so important to her, maybe it was because she felt she had to win twice—once for herself, and once for Noodle.

"If you feel that way," she replied stiffly, "Maybe you'd prefer it if we didn't see each other for a while."

Behind the brick wall of her defenses, Alex didn't feel nearly as strong and independent as she was making herself seem. She was scared and sad and hoped Danny would say something like, "Let's work it out, Alex. I love you too much not to try."

Instead, he only stared at her, not speaking, from behind the fence. His agonized expression mirrored her own emotions.

Finally, in a strangely hoarse voice, he said, "It's getting cold. You should put something on."

She wanted to scream, yell, shake the fence . . . but all she did was shrug. She wouldn't have noticed right now if the temperature were below zero; she felt completely numb.

"Danny . . ." she stopped, uncertain. She wanted to ask him if he would at least call her sometimes, but she couldn't even bring herself to do that.

He took a step backwards before turning away. "Good luck at the championship," he said stiffly.

Then quickly he walked off, striding up past the gym, his polo shirt becoming a blur of orange as the tears she'd been holding back welled up in her eyes.

"Does it make me look fat?" Lori posed in front of the three-way dressing room mirror in a yellow print bikini, her lovely face looking worried and uncertain. "I feel like an elephant!"

"You're about as fat as a stalk of celery," Kit told her. "In fact, you've been eating so much of it lately, I think you're probably turning into one."

Lori turned to Alex. "What do you think?"

Alex sighed. Lori looked sensational, as usual. Why couldn't she see it for herself? But, of course, she was too insecure. That's why she and Kit had agreed to go shopping with Lori, to help her pick out a new bikini for the Senior Picnic, which was going to be held up at Pineridge Lake this year. On her own, she probably would've picked a bathing suit that covered up all her imagined flaws—something that would resemble a circus tent.

"I think," she said, maintaining a deadpan expression, "that you'd better watch out if you plan to go swimming in that. One false move and every guy on the beach is going to jump in to rescue you."

Lori giggled. "Oh, Alex. Aren't you *ever* serious?"

"Not if I can help it."

The truth was, Alex felt miserable inside. She hadn't really talked to Danny since Saturday. Today was Friday, the day before the Sierra Club hiking trip. Almost a whole week. It seemed more like a year. Yet she went on, trying to pretend she was all right, holding in her misery. Crying out loud about it, she thought, would only have made it hurt worse.

Not even her friends guessed how bad she felt—to them she was still good old wisecracking Alex.

"I think these mirrors were invented for masochists," Lori complained. "How come the mirrors in department store dressing rooms always make you look like you weigh three hundred pounds?"

She'd seemed especially nervous about her looks, Alex reflected, since she'd learned that Perry Kingston would be riding up on their bus.

"Here, try on the other one," Kit suggested, holding up a scrap of metallic-blue material that was supposed to be a one-piece.

"We'd better hurry and decide," said Alex, glancing at the big waterproof watch she wore on her wrist. "We've been in here so long the saleslady is probably getting ready to call out the National Guard."

"That's just what you need," Kit said. "A whole army of men marching in here and telling you how gorgeous you look. Maybe *then* you'd believe it."

Lori's naturally pink color grew even pinker. "Come on, you guys, quit kidding around—I'm serious. How can I go to the picnic looking like this?"

"Like *what*?" Kit wanted to know.

Lori pressed a hand to her stomach, which looked perfectly flat to Alex. "Just look at this stomach! Everyone is going to think I'm pregnant!" She stopped as she caught sight of Kit's stricken expression. "Oh, Kit, I'm so sorry! Are you . . . have you . . ."

Kit shook her head. "I still don't know for sure yet," she said, lowering her voice as if she were afraid someone in the next dressing room might hear.

"Does Justin know?" Alex asked, filled with sympathy for what Kit must be going through.

"I haven't told him. I don't want him to know—until I'm sure, that is." Kit slumped down on the bench that was wedged into one corner of the tiny dressing room. "There's no point in getting him worried, too."

"Don't you think he'd *want* to know?" Lori asked hesitantly. "I mean, if he's the father—" she stopped herself, bringing her hands to her cheeks. "God, what am I saying? Oh, Kit, do you really think you could be pregnant?"

"This is crazy," Alex broke in, before Kit could answer. "Kit, you've got to *do* something!"

Kit had her head down, elbows planted on her knees, her chin cradled in her palms. She spoke to the floor. "I'm afraid to do anything," she confessed. "If I have to go down to Planned Parenthood and stand in some line with everybody looking at me and asking me a lot of questions I'll just *die*."

"What about those home tests they have?"

Lori said. "You know, the do-it-yourself kind. There's this girl in my PE class—she has the locker next to mine. Well, she left it open the other day and I happened to see one in there."

"I wonder if it worked," Alex remarked.

"It must have. She came to school the next day with her eyes all swollen from crying. I felt so sorry for her! I wanted to say something to make her feel better, but I was afraid she'd think I'd been snooping in her locker."

Kit sighed. "You're right. I suppose I should get it over with. It's just . . . I have this awful doomed feeling about the whole thing. Now I know how Marie Antoinette must've felt when she was on her way to the guillotine."

Lori ended up getting the yellow bikini after all. Then they all walked over to Rexall's, which was at the other end of the mall. Alex hooked her arm through Kit's for support. Kit looked like the sky had fallen in on her; she always wore her heart on her sleeve. In a way, Alex couldn't help wishing she were a little more like Kit, who never had a hard time expressing her emotions.

"It's not as bad as you think," she told Kit. "Justin really loves you. However it turns out, you won't have to go through it alone."

Unexpectedly, Alex felt a surge of pain. Did Danny love her the way Justin loved Kit? She'd believed so once . . . now she wasn't so sure. There were all kinds of love, she thought, like the different shades of the rainbow, but true-blue love was the rarest. It was the only kind that didn't evaporate when you ran into trouble. In fact, the more difficulties you were able to work out together, the stronger it got.

She'd seen it with her parents. Noodle's illness had brought them closer, even though she knew they didn't talk about it much to each other. A lot of CF parents, Dad had told her, get torn apart by the problem and end up getting divorced. It was like climbing a mountain, he said. You had to pull each other up a step at a time, and it never got any easier. . . .

She'd always thought it would be that way with Danny if they ever had a real problem. But apparently, she'd been wrong.

Kit seemed to read her mind. "Are you and Danny still not speaking?" she asked.

They walked slowly. Since it was a weekday, the mall was fairly uncrowded. There were a few shoppers sitting on the redwood benches that lined the concrete walkway, but it was such a nice day, nobody seemed to have much interest in staying inside.

"We talk to each other," Alex said cautiously, picking her way through the minefield of her own emotions. "We don't say much, though. You know, like 'Hi, how's it going?' and 'See you around.' " She fingered the gold chain she wore around her neck, which Danny had given her on her last birthday. Softly, she confessed,

96

"It hurts, you know. Sometimes I think it would be better if we just screamed at each other. The funny thing is, we always used to yell at each other when we argued—only it was always about dumb stuff that didn't really matter. Like that time Danny wanted me to go over to his grandmother's for some big family thing and I told him I didn't want to, because everybody in his family is always saying what an adorable couple we are—and I hate being adorable. I'm not the least bit adorable."

It was the worst fight they'd ever had up until now. They'd yelled at each other for ten minutes, but she'd gone anyway, even though she was still sort of mad. They had a huge dinner, and blueberry pie for dessert. Afterwards, she saw that Danny's teeth were blue and started to laugh. Then he broke up because he said hers were blue, too. Then they'd kissed, and Danny said her kiss tasted like blueberries. . . .

Alex shut her mind against that memory. There was a tight, stinging sensation behind her eyes. She willed herself not to cry, swallowing her tears before they could rise to the surface. They left a burning ache in the pit of her stomach. The only trouble was, there were so many memories. Each time she shut the door on one, she would remember something else.

"I know what you mean," Lori put in. "Some things are just too big for words." She wore a sad look, as if she really did know what Alex was talking about.

Kit slowed down even more as they approached the drug store. "I can't go through with it," she hissed. "What if someone recognizes me?"

Lori peered in through the big plate-glass window. "There's no one in there except the clerk and one old man. Come on, let's just get it over with." She looked almost as embarrassed as Kit, though Alex knew Lori would have walked over hot coals to help one of her friends.

Kit groaned. Her face was bright red as she ducked inside, flanked by Alex and Lori on either side. She got as far as the sanitary napkin aisle, then froze, refusing to go any farther. Alex followed her gaze, which was fixed on the shelf containing what she wanted—boxes marked "Early Pregnancy Test." They were behind the counter; she would have to ask the clerk to get her one.

"I *can't*," she muttered in panic. "Oh, God, how did I let you talk me into this?"

"Don't worry," Alex told her. "I'll get you out of it." She waited while the old man at the counter in front of them fumbled for his change, then she marched up in Kit's place.

She was embarrassed, too, but she decided the best thing to do was to act completely natural, as though buying a pregnancy test was something she did every day.

"Um, I'd like one of those," she said, pointing to the row of boxes.

The clerk, a sour-looking middle-aged woman with tight gray curls, frowned as she plucked one of the boxes off the shelf and banged it down next to the cash register. In pure defiance, Alex blurted, "*This* time I hope it's a boy."

The woman's disapproving expression turned to one of shock, her mouth dropping open. Alex suppressed the urge to burst into mad giggles. She dug the money out of the back pocket of her jeans, then snatched up her package and ran outside.

The three of them ran all the way out to Alex's old green Dodge without stopping once. They collapsed onto the seats, gasping for breath.

"I can't believe you said that," Lori choked, fighting to control her giggles.

"I don't know what made me do it," Alex said. "I guess I figured it was none of her business and she had no right judging me or anybody else."

Kit was staring at her with an incredulous expression. "You were so *brave*. I would've chickened out for sure."

"I'm not as brave as you think," she said, thinking of all the times she'd almost chickened out, too. "Just crazier, I guess." She turned the key in the ignition, and the engine started with a noisy rattle.

Kit squeezed her hand. "Thanks," she said softly, her big blue eyes full of gratitude. "I really owe you."

"Don't mention it," Alex said, a smile tugging at the corners of her mouth. "I just hope you never have to do the same for me someday."

After dropping off Kit and Lori, she stopped at Elaine's to return a Chemistry book she'd borrowed. Elaine lived in a big old Victorian filled with furniture, kids, and animals that looked like something out of Dr. Seuss. Mrs. Gregory greeted Alex at the door wearing an old shirt streaked with varnish—she was always refinishing something—and said that Elaine was up in her room studying.

Out of habit, Alex walked in without knocking. Elaine was sitting on her bed. She looked up at Alex with an expression of chagrined surprise, stuffing something she'd been holding under her pillow. Her cheeks flared with color.

"Alex!" she squeaked. "What are you doing here?"

"I said I was going to drop by, remember?" Alex peered at her. "What's going on—you'd think I was the FBI."

"Oh, I thought you were my sister. She *is* the FBI—only in her case, it stands for Forever Butting In." With a sheepish look, she fished out the object she'd hidden under her pillow.

It was some sort of weird contraption—two pieces of pink plastic held together with a big spring. Alex stared at it curiously. "I sent away for it," Elaine explained. "It just came in the mail today."

"What is it?" Alex asked.

"Promise you won't laugh?"

"If you knew what I'd just been through, you wouldn't even ask. Believe me, nothing you could tell me could be worse."

Elaine jumped up off her bed and locked the door. She came back over and sat down beside Alex, whispering, "It's a bust developer. You've seen those ads in the backs of magazines."

Alex had. They always showed a "before" picture of a girl in a bikini whose chest looked as if it had been stepped on by an elephant. In the "after" picture, supposedly taken about two weeks later, the same girl could pass for Dolly Parton. She couldn't believe Elaine had actually sent away for one of those things.

Elaine must have seen her expression, for she grinned ruefully. "I know what you're thinking. How dumb, right? Well, I know it won't make me look like Christie Brinkley, but I figured if it helped just a little, it would be worth it."

Alex didn't know what Elaine was so worried about. She was slender, but everything was in proportion. Besides, Elaine had never been as hung up about her body as Lori.

"Does this, by chance, have something to do with Carl?" she asked, suddenly struck with inspiration.

Elaine nodded, poking her glasses back into place. "I want to look good when he sees me in a bathing suit at the picnic."

Alex rolled her eyes. "You and Lori! The two of you should form a club: Insecure Anonymous. Of course, no one would know it to look at you. Think how many girls would kill to have your figure."

"It's not the girls I'm worried about," Elaine pointed out. "Honestly, if Carl doesn't do something pretty soon I'm going to develop a major insecurity complex. The last time we went out, he took me miniature golfing. True, he never really had a chance to kiss me since there were about fifty million people standing around, but the point is he *could* have taken me to the drive-in. Would you believe I've never even *been* to the drive-in with a boy? I'm the only teen-ager I know who actually goes to watch the movies."

Alex thought how ironic it was that Kit was so worried about the results of having gone too far, while Elaine was thinking she hadn't gone far enough. And here she was herself, stuck right in the middle with nowhere to go, since Danny was probably never going to ask her out again.

Life was so crazy.

"I'd watch out if I were you," she warned Elaine. "Sometimes when you wish for something, you really don't know what you're getting. What happens if you get Carl *too* steamed up?"

"I don't think that's very likely," Elaine said gloomily. "But I'll take my chances." She pointed at the bust developer with a grin peeking at the corners of her mouth. "Besides, there's a money-back guarantee if it doesn't work."

Alex sighed. "Too bad love doesn't come with a guarantee."

Chapter Eight

The house was quiet when Alex arrived home from practice late Saturday afternoon. Too quiet. She thought: *something is wrong*.

She knew what it was even before she saw the look on her mother's face as she walked into the living room.

"Where's Noodle?" she asked, catching sight of his empty chair near the hallway.

Her mother was sitting on the couch holding a cup of coffee that looked as if it had gone cold. She glanced up as Alex spoke.

"He's sleeping," she said. "Finally. He just wore himself out coughing. That cold of his is getting worse, I think." She put the cup down on the glass coffee table and got up, pacing over to the big picture window that looked out on the front garden and lawn. "Dr. Thompson says his lungs are deteriorating. I'm afraid he . . ." She stopped with a shudder. Bracing herself—Alex could see her shoulder blades pull back under her baby-blue cashmere sweater—she continued in a lighter voice, "Just look at those zinnias. I wonder if Miguel isn't giving them too much water. You know, too much water is just as bad for flowers as not enough. Why, they look half—" This time, she broke off with a little choking sound.

Alex wanted to comfort her mother somehow, but she kept her distance. It was a silent pact they had among them—Mom, Dad, and her. Each allowed the others to grieve in his or her own way. Part of the reason was not wanting to admit the truth—that Noodle was dying—at least, not aloud. Once something was spoken, there was no taking it back. Privately, they all knew what was happening, but to each other, and to Noodle, they pretended there was a chance that the doctors would be able to find a cure before it was too late.

The trouble was, if they couldn't talk to one another about it, whom *could* they talk to? No one else really understood what it was like to watch someone you love slip away from you a little more each day, even those who tried their best to be sympathetic. It wasn't the same as actually *being* there.

"I'll look in on him," Alex said, knowing the best thing to do was to leave Mom alone right now.

Noodle was asleep, but when she tiptoed in, his eyes opened. He lay propped up on a mound of pillows wearing the prongs that fed oxygen through a tube into his nose to help him breathe better. He blinked, trying to focus on her, then gave a faint smile.

"Hi," she said. "I heard you were sick. Faking it again, huh?"

Laughter rattled up from his chest, but that only got him started coughing again. He coughed so violently, Alex grew frightened for a moment. She sat down on the bed and put her arms around him. He was so thin! She could feel the knobs of his spine sticking out. She thought of a baby bird she'd once rescued when it fell out of its nest, and how she'd known just looking at that tiny, gray, featherless lump that it couldn't possibly survive. She had that same feeling now and had to bite the inside of her mouth to keep from crying.

"If you think this is good, you should stick around for the finale," he whispered hoarsely once he'd gotten himself under control. He grinned—a ghastly imitation grin.

"You have a morbid sense of humor," she said, though she knew that the jokes they both made were only a way of easing the awful tension. Still, she felt as if someone had jabbed a needle into her chest. Her heart ached.

"I know. I must've gotten it from you. Mom and Dad never joke around much, have you noticed? Sometimes, I wonder—well, if I hadn't been born, maybe they would have been happier." His expression grew serious. "You know what I mean?"

"Of course they wouldn't be," she said angrily. "That's just . . . *dumb*."

He settled back against his pillows with a deep sigh. "No, it isn't. I've thought about it a lot. I'm not saying they *wish* I'd never been born. What I mean is, they'd probably be happier if I hadn't been, that's all. I guess it's not easy having a kid who's sick all the time."

Typical Noodle, she thought. He often worried more about the pain he caused others than his own. Suddenly, she was struck by a bolt of love so powerful, it hurt.

"You think too much, you know that," she scolded gruffly. "It comes from being too smart for your own good." She reached over and ruffled his hair, making it stand up in stiff black spikes.

"I've been thinking a lot about what it's like to die," he said softly. "I wonder if there's such a thing as Heaven. I wonder if believing in Heaven is like believing in Santa Claus."

"I don't think it's the same thing," she said. "Heaven is . . . well, you've *got* to believe in Heaven, or what else is there?"

"When I was real little, I thought it would be like in picture books—you know, up in the clouds with some white-bearded guy sitting on a throne, and a bunch of angels with harps. Now I think, if there is a Heaven, it must be more a feeling than a place . . . like going to sleep and dreaming good things."

He wore a far-off expression that pinched at her heart. *He was so pale*, she thought. *How had he managed to get so sick without her noticing? He'd had this cold for the last week or so, but she'd been so busy with practice . . .*

"I'll probably get there first at the rate I'm going," she teased gently. "I'll send you a postcard when I get there to let you know how it is. I'll write, 'Having a great time. Wish you were here.' "

He smiled. It was a weak smile, but a genuine one. "Thanks a lot. I'll look forward to it."

She pressed his hand, smiling hard to keep from crying. "Listen, you're going to get better, you hear?"

He blinked. "What makes you think so?"

"Because! Because I said so, that's why. Because for some dumb reason I happen to like having you around." Her voice faltered. "See what you did? You made me cry, and you know how much I hate crying." Furious with herself, she swiped at her cheeks with the back of her hand.

"It's okay," he said. "You can cry."

"It's *not* okay." She jumped up off the bed, turning to face the wall.

When Noodle was born, her father had put up the kind of wallpaper he thought would be perfect for a boy's room: blue with a design of football players. Now, as Alex stared at all those little football players swimming around in front of her, she thought how awful it must be for Noodle, day after day, to lie here and be reminded of all the things he couldn't do. Funny, how she never really noticed it before.

After she'd gotten herself under control, she turned back to Noodle. His eyes were closed. He had fallen asleep. The only sound was the awful wheezing of his oxygen pump. She tiptoed out and shut the door.

The sound of her father playing the piano drifted in from the living room. Alex hesitated in the hallway. She wanted so badly to talk to someone. Dad would have understood the way she felt.

He was playing something very intense and emotional—Liszt, she guessed. Her father had been a concert pianist before he went to medical school. The reason he'd quit playing professionally, he'd once told her, was because he'd known that, although he was good, he would never be one of the *best*.

Now he played mostly for his own enjoyment, or when he was especially keyed up about something. When he was sad or depressed, he usually played something stormy and emotional like Liszt or Chopin. During those times, he was off in his own world, like a sailor lost at sea. It was no use trying to talk to him now, she realized.

Instead, Alex crept into her bedroom. She shut the door and stretched out on the bed, letting the music fill her up as if she were an empty shell. That's the way she felt—as if someone had come along and scooped out all her insides, leaving only this awful, aching emptiness. Having lost Danny, she knew what it was like to lose someone you love. It was . . . well, a little like dying yourself, only there was no Heaven afterwards.

She thought of Danny hiking up into the mountains without her and felt a wave of regret. Would it really have made that much of a difference if she'd skipped practice today to go with him? Maybe she should have gone. . . .

Then her thoughts turned to Noodle, lying there in that bed, and she knew she'd done the right thing. She couldn't let him down. She had to win. She just *had* to.

Chapter Nine

The championship was being held in San Jose this year, two hours from Glenwood. Alex drove over with her coach and John Nylander, while her father followed in the family station wagon with Kit, Elaine, and Lori. Her mother had wanted to come, but decided at the last minute to stay with Noodle, whose cold hadn't gotten any better. It was much worse, in fact.

Alex felt thankful, though, that her friends had managed to swing it. She knew it hadn't been easy for them. Kit had cancelled out on a Saturday afternoon dance recital, Lori skipped work, and Elaine had made the biggest sacrifice of all—she'd turned down a date with Carl. What would she do without her friends? Alex wondered.

By the time they arrived, she was so nervous she could barely speak. Both John and Coach Reeves had coached her on the way over, going over once again all the things the judges would be looking for. They were encouraging, but her confidence withered when she saw the crowd of people and the Olympic-sized pool. Some of the best people in the whole state would be competing here today—how could she hope to win? She was crazy to have ever thought she'd be good enough . . .

Kit, Lori, and Elaine crowded into the locker room beforehand to offer her moral support.

"I'd place my bets on you," Kit said, adding with a wry grimace, "if I had any money, that is."

She appeared to be in good spirits, Alex observed, even though her period still hadn't come. The do-it-yourself test had turned out negative, she'd told them, but that didn't necessarily mean she could stop worrying. According to the instructions that had come with the kit, taking the test too early in the pregnancy could have a negative result. So, Kit was still chewing her nails, waiting to see what would happen.

"You're the best," Elaine told her. "I know you're going to win. I'm not even nervous about it, and you know how nervous *I* get sometimes."

Alex wished she were as confident, but she didn't tell her friends how nervous she was. They expected her to be self-assured, so she didn't want to let them down. Even so, she longed to say how she felt. It was such a strain, keeping all her fears to herself, trying to act perfect all the time. But what would people think if they knew the truth? If they could see all the cracks in her armor?

"I'll be okay," she said, forcing a grin. "I'll just pretend it's one more practice session, with Coach Reeves waiting to chew me out if I mess up. That's my good luck charm."

Lori hugged her. "Good luck, anyway, Alex. I know you won't need it, but a little extra never hurts."

Alex spent the next half hour warming up by swimming laps in the pool. A few of the other divers—she recognized Virginia Kirk's distinctive red-and-yellow cap—were practicing dives, but John and her coach had both felt she should save her strength for the actual competition. She knew they were right. She was a good diver, but it was her fierce competitiveness that gave her the winning edge.

She only wished Danny could be here. She hadn't realized until now how much she'd counted on his supportiveness. Often, he didn't even have to say anything. It was enough just to look over and see him smiling at her. . . .

What made the whole thing even worse was the fact that she was also furious with him. This was probably the most important moment of her life. Even if he no longer wanted to be her boyfriend, couldn't he have at least shared it with her? She knew her triumph, if she won, wouldn't be the same without Danny, and that made her even angrier.

Okay, Danny, I'll win without you, she told herself through gritted teeth.

There were ten required dives in all: five compulsories and the rest combinations, which had been filed with the judges earlier. Alex knew that if, for some reason, she didn't complete any of her combinations, she couldn't receive a score higher than two points for that dive. Her toughest dive was a reverse one-and-a-half layout with a two-and-a-half twist. It was almost never done in competition, John told her, because it was so difficult. Alex even remembered reading about some woman who had broken her arm trying it in the Olympics one year.

The competition was being held in a special diving pool with a three-meter springboard and a ten-meter platform. The judges sat at separate tables lined up along the right-hand edge of the pool. Row after row of bleachers rose up on the other side. The announcer was a tall, gray-haired woman dressed in white, like the judges. Over her microphone she announced the name of the first competitor. Alex was up second for the compulsories.

She wasn't too worried about the compulsories; those were the easy dives. Shutting her mind against the sea of faces watching her, she breezed through them, scoring well enough to place at the top coming into the final leg. Virginia Kirk fell to third place. Second went to a twenty-year-old girl from Los Angeles named Karen Grossman.

Alex was thrilled, but she knew the hard part was still to come. She didn't dare allow herself to relax or grow overconfident.

"Miss Alex Enomoto will now be executing a forward somersault with a one-and-a-half twist," the gray-haired woman announced. "The degree of difficulty of the dive is two-point-five. . . ."

Her heart was in her throat as she mounted the board. If she blew it now . . .

But her luck held out. She executed the dive perfectly, entering the water with good, straight form, hardly making a splash.

She was watching Virginia execute a difficult backward dive when, out of the corner of her eye, she saw her coach signal to her. Alex trotted over to where he stood. That was when she noticed her father, too. Both men wore concerned looks.

Her father took her aside. "I just talked to your mother. . . ."

She knew even before he told her. It was as if she had a sixth sense where her brother was concerned. She shivered in her thin nylon racing suit, hugging her arms against her chest as if to ward off a blow.

". . . Noodle's in the hospital. It happened about an hour after we left. One of his lungs collapsed." Her father's face was white and strained. She'd never seen him look so worried.

"How bad?" Alex wanted to know. Dad would level with her; he always had in the past.

"I don't know. She sounded pretty upset. I think I should get up there as quickly as possible. You know how much I was counting on being with you, honey, but . . ."

Alex felt as if she'd had the wind knocked out of her. Her head was spinning, and she was having a hard time breathing. She wanted to be with Noodle, too, but . . .

Everything she'd hoped for . . . dreamed of . . . all of it gone if she left now. She would be instantly disqualified, and she'd lose John Nylander as a coach forever.

Alex cast an agonized look at her father, but he only shook his head. "It's up to you, Alex," he said. "I can't make that decision for you." Alex glanced over at the diving area; her turn was coming up next.

Suddenly, she knew what she had to do. It struck her with such force that she wondered how she could have even hesitated for a moment. Danny was right. She *had* allowed her own ambition to overshadow the things that were really important in her life. Nothing, she realized, was more important than her own family.

A wave of shame swept over her at what she'd almost done. What if she'd lost her last chance to see Noodle? She had to face the fact that he could be dying at this very minute. She might have stayed until the end of the competition . . . and by the time she got to the hospital it might have been too late. How would she have felt about winning then?

She thought of Noodle lying in his hospital bed. He hated it when he had to go to the hospital, even though he'd made some good friends among the doctors and nurses. He joked that he'd had so many needles stuck in him he could double as a pincushion, but Alex knew he only joked because he was so miserable. He needed her now more than ever. And she'd come so close to letting him down.

She gave her father a long look. "I'll get my things."

Alex almost cried when she saw him. He looked so small, stretched out like a reed under the thin white blanket that covered him. She wondered how they'd managed to find enough of him to stick all those tubes into. There were tubes running out of his nose, his arm, his chest.

She sat down gingerly on the end of the bed.

He opened his eyes and smiled. *At least they haven't taken that away*, she thought.

"Mom and Dad are outside," she told him. "They said I could come in alone." Her mouth felt as if it were full of cotton when she spoke.

Noodle tried to talk, but could only manage a whisper. She could see how hard it was for him even to breathe. "Did you win?" he wanted to know.

Alex shook her head. She willed herself not to cry. "Are you kidding? Did you think I'd want to hang around winning prizes when I could be visiting you in this fantastic place?"

"You disqualified yourself?" His eyes were like black pools in the still whiteness of his face. "Because of me? That was dumb."

"Yeah, well, acting dumb is just one of my many talents." She played with a corner of the sheet, rolling it between her thumb and forefinger. "Anyway, I *would* have won. You should have seen me. I was terrific."

"I'll bet. Look, the truth is, I'm the one who feels dumb. I picked a dumb time to get sick."

"Don't say that. It wasn't your fault. Oh, Noodle . . . I *wanted* to win . . . for both of us. . . ."

"Both of us?" he echoed in confusion.

It all came out in a gush. "I've always felt that way—like I had to win for both of us. I . . . I've always felt guilty that . . . that you were the one born with CF and not me. It's not fair. I have everything and you . . ." she clapped a hand over her mouth to stifle the cry of anguish that rose up inside her.

He turned his head slowly against the pillow, as if it were agony for him just to move that tiniest bit. "You're wrong," he said. "I have a lot. I have a wonderful family and people who love me. Isn't that what really counts?"

She nodded silently. She no longer cared if anyone saw her cry. Let them, she thought, as the tears spilled down her cheeks.

"Don't win for me," he continued, "Win for yourself. I don't want what you have. I'm not so unlucky. Hey, what are you crying for?"

"I'm not crying," she choked. "The sun's in my eyes. It makes them water."

He tried to grin, but it was too much of an effort. His gaze was on the window that overlooked the parking lot. "It's practically dark outside."

"Yeah, well, I have sensitive eyes."

He closed his own eyes and was quiet for such a long time that she thought he'd gone to sleep. There was even a moment when his chest seemed to stop moving, and her heart lurched in fear. Then his eyes opened again and his hand moved across the blanket to touch hers.

"I'm not coming home this time," he said softly . . . so softly she had to bend close in order to hear him. "Don't tell them I said so. It'll only make it worse for them." She didn't have to ask who "them" were. She knew he meant Mom and Dad. He was protecting them . . . as he always had.

Alex knew it was time to let him talk. There was no point in hiding from the truth any longer. Noodle needed to be honest, and it would have been selfish of her to run away now.

"I love you," she said, surprised at how easy it was.

His eyes shone with a brightness that was beyond tears. "Sometimes . . . I get so afraid. Remember what we talked about before? Well, I'm afraid maybe there really isn't a Heaven. Maybe it's like getting swallowed up into this great big dark hole."

"No, I'm sure it's not like that." She squeezed his hand as hard as she dared. He seemed so brittle, as if his bones were made of glass. "Remember when we were little and used to pretend that if we reached up high enough we could catch a star? Well, I think you're just a little bit closer than I am, that's all. One of these days, I'll catch up."

He managed a small smile. "Hey, that'll be a first. Me getting somewhere ahead of you."

"You can't win 'em all, I guess."

Tears dripped off her chin to the backs of their entwined hands. She ached with sadness, but at the same time she felt strangely relieved to be talking with him this way. It would have been so much worse, letting him go without saying good-bye.

"I'll miss you," he said. "Wherever I'm going . . . it won't be the same without you."

"Yeah, I know. I feel the same way."

He closed his eyes again with a sigh. "One more thing. I'm glad you came . . . even if it was dumb. I wanted you to win, but I'm glad you came."

"So am I," she said, knowing it was the truth.

Chapter Ten

Alex had prayed that Noodle would die in his sleep so he wouldn't know it was coming and be afraid. When the phone rang at three o'clock on Tuesday morning, she knew her prayer had been answered.

The funeral was on Wednesday. She spent the morning in the field behind her house picking wild flowers. Noodle would've hated the great big ugly spray of chrysanthemums they put on his coffin, she thought. He hated anything that looked artificial or imprisoned.

The field sloped up into a hill which no one ever climbed because it was a tangle of weeds and old blackberry vines that looked like rusty barbed wire. Alex climbed it anyway, letting the brambles tear at her clothes and scratch her skin. In fact, it felt good in a strange way. Since yesterday, she'd been numb, unable to feel anything. Even pain, she decided, was better than nothing.

At the top of the hill, she held her bouquet up, letting the wind tear at the tops of the dandelion puffs. She watched the tiny feathers of white fluff swirl up into the sky, remembering how she always used to make a wish whenever she blew on one. She didn't have to make a wish now. Noodle was free. Nothing could hurt him again.

She stayed up on the hill until her tears had dried into trails of salt. Until it was time to go. She climbed down the hill more slowly than she'd gone up, picking her way carefully through the brambles.

Back at the house, she changed into a dark green skirt and navy-blue sweater. She refused to wear black. Then she and her parents rode over to the chapel together.

No one spoke in the car. Her mother looked as if she were in a daze. She just stared out the window. Alex noticed she was wearing her black herringbone suit, but her shoes were brown. It was the first time she could remember her mother's shoes not being color coordinated to match her outfit. Her dad, she saw, had put on a pair of very dark sunglasses, even though it was a cloudy day. He didn't say anything, either, but as they were going into the chapel, he held her hand tightly.

Alex herself felt numb. She'd cried so much since yesterday, she felt all dried up inside. But as soon as she saw Kit, Elaine, and Lori, her eyes filled up again.

Kit was the first to walk over and put her arms around Alex. "If you need me . . . for anything . . . I'm here," she murmured.

Alex could only nod in gratitude. There was a huge lump inside her throat and she knew if she tried to speak, it would overflow.

Lori was crying enough for all four of them. Strands of hair clung to her wet cheeks after she'd finished hugging Alex.

"Oh, Alex . . . I'm so s-s-sorry," she choked.

Elaine's big glasses were misted over, too, she saw, though it was obvious she was making an attempt not to cry. She squeezed Alex's hand tightly. "I loved him, too," she said.

Alex knew it was true. Elaine had considered Noodle to be the closest thing to a brother she had. She remembered all the times Elaine had visited Noodle in the hospital. The three of them used to sit on his bed playing Scrabble until visiting hours were over and one of the nurses kicked them out. Noodle had loved Elaine, too.

The service was short. At least, it seemed that way to Alex, who barely heard a word of it. Afterwards, they rode out to the grave site.

She couldn't watch as they lowered the coffin into the ground. She covered her face. It was the only time throughout the entire ordeal when she cried. Noodle was really gone. She would never see him again. They would never tease each other. He would never beat her at chess. She would never tell him stories.

Once upon a time, there was a boy named Noodle . . .

When she looked up again, she saw Danny standing a short distance away, beside a row of stunted pine trees planted to block out the parking lot. At first she didn't know it was he. It was the first time she'd ever seen him wearing a suit and tie. Their eyes met. His looked red, as if he'd been crying, too.

Alex quickly looked away. The dull ache inside her flowered into a razor-sharp pain. It was too much. She couldn't bear being reminded of that other loss, too.

"Alex—" He caught up with her as she was leaving. He tried to put his arms around her, but she pulled away. Part of her wanted nothing more than for him to hold her, to blot out her pain with the warmth of his embrace, but she wouldn't give in to that feeling. It would only make things worse for her in the end.

"You were right," Alex said, looking down at the grass. She knew that if she looked him in the eyes, she would start crying all over again.

"No, that's what I wanted to tell you. It doesn't matter. I love you the way you are. I shouldn't have tried to change you. If I did that, you wouldn't be . . . well, *you*." Danny gripped her shoulders. "I know this isn't the time, but . . . can we talk later?"

The grass was wet. She stared down at the flattened impressions their footprints had made. She didn't know what to say. She didn't know how to tell him that she had changed. She wasn't the same Alex anymore. No longer a winner. What was the good of winning, if you couldn't have what was really important?

Finally, she allowed herself to look up. Danny was crying, his blue eyes blurred with tears.

"I'll call you," he said softly, letting go of her shoulders.

She didn't answer. She just walked away. Danny had belonged to the old Alex. She couldn't speak for this new stranger she'd become. She didn't know what her feelings were anymore.

Except that she felt like dying, too.

Chapter Eleven

"You might as well get up," Kit warned, her blue eyes flashing as she stood over Alex. "We're making you come even if we have to tie you up and kidnap you."

Alex didn't budge. She lay in her bed, hanging on to her crumpled sheets as though they were a lifeline. She'd been in bed for more than a week. She'd told everyone she had the flu, but the truth was she just hadn't been able to think of a good enough reason for getting up.

"Forget it," she mumbled, burrowing back under the covers. "The world will survive if I don't go to the Senior Picnic."

"Maybe so," Elaine said, "but, will *you*? How much longer do you think you can go on hiding out in here?"

Lori sat down beside her on the bed. "I know how you must feel," she said gently. "Even if I don't have a brother. But do you really think this is what Noodle would have wanted? He was a fighter—just like you."

"I'm not a fighter anymore," Alex said. "I don't care about winning. I don't care about anything."

She inched her way down until she could pull the covers all the way over her head. The sheets smelled of stale perspiration, and Alex knew she probably smelled, too. She hadn't taken a shower or washed her hair in a week. But it didn't matter. Nothing mattered. She would stay this way, inside her dark cocoon, forever.

Suddenly, sunlight exploded into the room. She jerked upright, squinting her eyes against the brilliance. Kit was standing by the drapes, cord in hand.

"Ow, it hurts!" Alex cried out. It was the first time the sun had been let into her room since Noodle's funeral.

"I know," Kit said. "A lot of things hurt. You can't run away from them all. Sometimes you have to let something hurt before it can heal."

Kit was wearing a pair of tight white shorts and a Hawaiian-print midriff top. Her tousled wheat-gold hair was caught up on top of her head with an array of rainbow-colored combs. She had her hands on her hips as if she were prepared to do battle.

"Kit's right," Elaine said. "You should go, even if you don't want to. You might not have a terrific time, but you'll feel better afterwards."

"No I won't," Alex answered defiantly. She didn't *want* to have a good time. She didn't want to feel better. Noodle was dead. How could she ever have fun again, knowing that?

Lori's wide blue eyes misted over in sympathy. Lori understood, Alex thought. She'd lost her father.

"You're the one who's always telling us you have to go on even when you feel like you can't," Lori said. "We're just giving you your own advice."

She was wearing an apricot-colored sundress and a big straw hat. She looked like a movie star, Alex thought. As for herself, she knew she probably looked like the Bride of Frankenstein. It was the first time in a week that she'd thought about what she must look like.

"Go away!" she cried, yanking her pillow over her face. "Go to the picnic without me! Just leave me alone!"

But Kit remained stubborn. "Nothing doing. We're not leaving you here to rot away. We love you! We're trying to help you. Now are you going to get up, or are we going to have to drag you out of that bed?"

Elaine grabbed one of her arms, giving it a gentle tug to show she meant business. Alex tried to squirm away, but all the time she'd spent in bed not exercising had taken its toll. She was shocked at how weak she was.

"Having friends is like being married in a way," Elaine said. "That means we stick together through thick and thin. Till death do us part."

Alex started to cry. She pressed her face into the pillow, sobbing out her anguish in big, noisy, aching gusts. She felt a hand stroking her back.

Finally, she lifted her head. "Okay," she snuffled, "I'll go. But don't expect me to have a good time."

Alex sat in the back of the bus on the ride up to Pineridge Lake. She refused to join in the conversation, no matter how hard her friends coaxed her. She didn't have the heart to do anything more than stare out the window. It was a beautiful sunny day, made-to-order picnic weather, but she couldn't appreciate even that.

At the lake, she hung back from the others, spreading her towel under a pine tree that stood up on a knoll overlooking the beach. Through a huge pair of sunglasses, she watched everybody else have a good time.

A group of kids were playing around in the water, splashing each other and doing cannonballs off the dock. She spotted Elaine and Carl a little farther out. Elaine was floating lazily on a plastic raft, with Carl swimming along beside her. Alex thought she looked very sexy in her new striped one-piece, though she couldn't see that the bust developer had made any difference. She doubted if Carl had, either. But it didn't matter; he seemed to have eyes only for Elaine.

Kit and Justin were walking up the beach, holding hands and talking quietly. Alex felt a small stab of guilt. She'd been so wrapped up in her own misery, she hadn't given a thought to Kit's dilemma this past week. She didn't even know if Kit had gotten her period yet. She hoped so. Even though she didn't care what happened to herself anymore, she certainly cared what happened to her friends.

She looked around for Lori, but didn't see her right away. When she finally spotted her, she realized why Lori had been so hard to find. Lori had been hiding, too—from a dark-haired boy who was attempting to make conversation with her. He fit the description of Perry Kingston, that boy from her old school whom she'd been avoiding. Lori sat on her towel with her knees tucked up against her chest and her big straw hat pulled down so that it covered half her face. She didn't look as though she were having a very good time at this moment.

Alex looked up as a shadow fell across her. Danny was standing over her. He'd ridden up in the other bus, so she hadn't seen him until now. Her heart leaped. He looked so handsome in his light-blue swim trunks, his tanned

131

shoulders glistening with droplets of water.

"I called," he said. "About a hundred times. Your mother said you were sick." He dropped down beside her, putting his hand on her knee. "Are you okay?"

She shrugged. "It depends on what you call okay," she said. "If you mean am I still alive— the answer is yes. If you mean, am I back to normal . . . no, I don't think I'll ever be back to normal." She looked at him squarely. "I made a decision this past week. I'm quitting the team. I'm giving up diving."

"You can't do that," he said. "Alex, I know how terrible you must feel about your brother, but do you really think that's what he would've wanted?"

"I don't know. He's not around for me to ask."

"Alex. Don't do this. Please. It's not like you. You've never been a quitter."

"I've changed. I just don't want to compete anymore. I don't care about winning. What's the use? I've already lost everything that's really important to me."

"You've got it all wrong. It's like I tried to tell you before. Winning's not the point. You compete because you want to, because something inside keeps pushing you to the limit of what you can do. It doesn't matter whether or not you're better than everybody else. It only matters if you're as good as *you* can be." He took her hand. "I think that's what your brother was all about, too. He accepted how he was, I could tell just by looking at him. He didn't want to be you. And I don't think he would've wanted you to be him."

Alex couldn't speak. That old lump was rising in her throat again. She fought to control it. She didn't want to cry in front of Danny now. It was too painful. She just wanted to crawl back into her hole. She was sorry she'd come.

"Danny, I . . . I don't want to talk about it. I've made up my mind. Please."

"Okay. Let's talk about something else then."

"What?"

"How about us?"

"I thought it was over with us."

"So did I. I didn't want it to be, though. I still don't. I missed you, Alex. I missed you so much I"—he looked down at the ground with a sheepish expression—"oh, hell, you might as well know, I didn't go on the hike like I planned. I stayed home and climbed the walls instead."

A tiny smile crept into the corners of her mouth. "I did a lot of that, too."

"Hey, do you want something to eat? They're setting up the barbeque now. You look like you haven't eaten in a week."

"You're right, I haven't," she said. She

hadn't felt hungry all week, but suddenly it hit her—she was ravenous.

He stood up, pulling her with him. "We've got to keep our strength up for the tug-of-war. Even though you're not on my team, I'm looking out for you. Sort of a self-appointed coach, you might say."

Alex had forgotten all about the tug-of-war. It was a Senior Picnic tradition at Glenwood High. The whole class had been divided up into two teams. They'd be pulling against each other on a rope as big around as her arm.

"Thanks, anyway," she said, "But I think I'll sit it out. I don't really feel up to it."

"Don't you care if your team wins or not?"

"If you want to know the truth—not really. I'm sorry, Danny, that's just the way I feel."

Danny's face tightened. "I think what you're really feeling is sorry for yourself."

"That's not true!" She felt as though he'd slapped her.

"Sure it is. If you ask me, I think it's a pretty lousy way to remember your brother. *He* never went around feeling sorry for himself."

Heat flooded her entire body.

"Who asked you for your crummy opinion, anyway?" she shouted back at him. "I hate you!"

"Good. I'm glad you can feel something other than self-pity."

Alex couldn't believe he was talking to her

this way. Her temples pounded with fury as she jumped to her feet. "You don't know how I feel! You don't have any idea! Nobody does!"

"Show me then. Don't be a quitter."

"I don't have to prove anything to you!"

"Then prove it to yourself. I think maybe you're afraid. You're afraid you *won't* be a winner, and you're using your brother as an excuse to drop out."

Her cheeks burned as if they'd been slapped. "I hate you, I really hate you!" she screamed, so loudly that a few heads turned toward them to see what all the commotion was about. "Besides that, you're wrong. I'll show you. I'll show you how wrong you are!"

When Alex saw that Danny had been placed at the head of the line on his side of the rope, she marched up and defiantly took the lead on hers. There were about fifty people on each end. The rope, strung out along the water's edge so that the losing team would have to fall in, seemed to stretch on forever like some kind of mammoth centipede.

Kit, who was directly behind her, hissed excitedly in her ear, "Way to go, Alex! With you on our side, we can't miss."

Actually, Alex wasn't too sure of that. She thought she was probably too out of shape to beat anyone, though she was certainly mad enough to try. Danny had no right to say those awful things to her, especially since he was the one who had pointed out how wrong she'd been in the first place to be so single-minded about winning. Well, this wasn't exactly the Olympics, but she'd show him she wasn't quitting just because she was afraid of not being good enough!

Chris Bowden, the class president, wasn't competing because of a sprained ankle, so he appointed himself the referee. He hobbled over to where his clothes were, fishing around for something in the pocket of his jeans. Then he pulled out a firecracker and a book of matches. He was grinning.

"Okay, guys, let's get this going with a real bang!" With that, he lit the firecracker, setting off the competition with a gunshot explosion.

Danny's team got in the first yank, nearly jerking Alex's arms from her sockets. She shot him a fierce look. He didn't flinch. He was facing her head-on, his hands clenched about the rope, the muscles in his arms and chest rippling with tension.

Alex pulled with all her strength, bending backwards with the effort. Damn him! He was grinning at her! Even though her arms trembled, she wouldn't quit. She could hear Kit groaning behind her.

"Help! My arms feel like they're going to fall off!" someone farther down the line cried.

A girl behind Danny fell out of line and tumbled laughing into the water. Someone else followed suit.

Alex could feel her body grow warm and damp with sweat. She was sorry now she hadn't worn her bathing suit. She was dressed in jeans and a T-shirt because she hadn't expected to be doing anything very active. Her T-shirt was stuck to her in large, wet patches. Only her feet were bare. She dug her heels into the muddy lake bottom, ignoring the pebbles that cut into her flesh.

Danny was sweating, too, she noticed with grim satisfaction. Strands of blond hair were plastered across his forehead, and tiny rivulets of perspiration trickled down his temples.

Whenever it seemed as if her side were gaining ground, Danny's side would pull just a little bit harder, winning back what they'd lost. Alex felt as if she'd been straining against the rope for hours, though it couldn't have been more than five minutes or so. Her palms were raw from rubbing against the rough hemp. The water she was immersed in up to her ankles had turned from clear blue to a muddy brown.

Oddly enough, she realized she was enjoying herself. Her whole body ached with the effort, but it was a good ache. Just as Danny had said . . . she was pressing herself to her own limit, and that's all that mattered . . .

Realizing he was right, however, made her that much madder at him. He was still grinning, although he didn't look quite as cocky as before. She saw that his expression had become more of a grimace.

Okay, Danny, you asked for it.

"Everybody . . . PULL!" she screamed at the top of her lungs.

It worked. They were moving backwards with Danny's side skidding toward them. Everybody on both sides was screaming. There was a loud bang as another firecracker went off.

Then suddenly, the rope seemed to give way and Alex tumbled into the water along with everybody else. She fell against someone, not knowing who it was until Danny's arms closed around her, pulling her free of the thrashing, wet jumble of bodies. She screamed and kicked, but he only held her closer, pinning her arms against her sides as they rolled over and over in the shallow, muddy water.

"I hate you!" she spluttered through a mouthful of water.

"I love you!" he yelled back. "You're just too stupid to know it."

"Who are you calling stupid, Stupid?"

Suddenly, they were both laughing so hard they had to stop. They lay in the water, gasping for breath. Danny was a mess—all streaked with mud and sand. He gave her a wet kiss, which she felt all the way to the soles of her feet. She sat there, staring at him in astonishment, too stunned to move.

"Come on, Ace, let's get you into some dry clothes," he said, hauling her up with him as he stood up in a cascade of muddy water.

"I don't have any," she said. "These are the only ones I brought."

"No sweat." He grinned. "I know a great place we can hike to from here where we won't need any at all. You want to?"

She read the message in his eyes, and nodded. She didn't know exactly when it had happened, but she knew she'd come alive again. She ached all over, but underneath a sweet warmth flowed through her. She felt as if she'd won something very important, though she had no idea what it was.

She raced ahead of him, running up the beach. When she got to the path that wound up into the woods, she called back to him through cupped palms, "Hey, slowpoke, what are you waiting for?"

Chapter Twelve

"I'm sorry about all those things I said,"
Danny told her, holding her hand as they
walked among the trees. "I didn't really mean
them. I was just trying to get you mad at me so
you'd stop being mad at yourself."

Alex looked up at him in surprise. "What
made you think I was mad at myself?"

"I had this friend in the fifth grade—did I
ever tell you about Bobby Stryker? Well, he was
my best friend. We did everything together
until he got sick. They found out he had
leukemia. Then he . . . well, he died. I guess I
don't like to talk about it much, because that
was a bad time for me. I felt terrible because
he'd died and nothing had happened to me. I
felt, I don't know, responsible somehow—even
though I know that sounds dumb."

"No, it doesn't," she said softly. "That's how I
feel. It doesn't seem fair, does it? I mean, all
along it seemed as if I was getting all the good

breaks . . . and Noodle kept ending up with the bad ones."

"I'm sure he wasn't looking at it that way."

"No, he is . . . wasn't like that." She looked up at Danny and smiled. "You know something? This is the first time I've really been able to talk about him since he died. It hurts, but I think it actually hurts less when you let it out, even though you feel it more. Does that make sense?"

"In a funny way . . . yeah. I know what you mean. When you cry about something, or get mad and yell, then it's over with. But when you hold it inside, it just gets worse, and you end up making yourself sick."

They'd climbed high enough now so that the lake was a silvery blue shimmer in the distance. The trees were thicker up here, and the path narrower. Every few minutes, they had to stop and clear away a dead branch or an overgrown vine before they could go on. The trail led up to the stream that fed the lake; they could hear it—a low, rustling sound—even though they couldn't see it yet.

The sun had dried Alex's clothes; they felt stiff and scratchy against her skin. Little bits of dried mud kept flaking off at every step. When they finally reached the stream, stopping at a quiet pool nestled among the rocks, the first thing she did was yank her T-shirt off. Underneath, she wore only her bra. But she was struck by a sudden need to feel the warm sun against her bare skin. Closing her eyes, she threw up her arms, letting the cool tingly spray tossed up by a tiny waterfall dance across her chest.

Alex felt Danny's warm arms slip around her from behind. He just held her like that for several minutes, not trying to kiss her. He seemed to know that what she needed most at this moment was just the comfort of his nearness. They stood there, listening to the whispery tumble of the water, and the pine needles swishing in the breeze.

"When I think of Noodle being in Heaven . . . I think of this," she said at last. "It's so perfect, isn't it? When I picture it this way, I can believe that maybe he really is much happier now." She slid around so that she was facing him. "I guess I *was* punishing myself, wasn't I? I was hiding out, making myself miserable to even the score somehow, so I wouldn't have to feel so guilty."

"How do you feel now?" he asked, smoothing her hair back from her face.

"Better. A little sadder, too, maybe—because when you talk about someone being dead, you're admitting it's really true. I guess I was sort of putting that part off as long as I could."

"It's easy to understand why you would want to. Your brother was a terrific guy. He was really special."

142

Alex put her head on his chest, resting her cheek against the smooth swell of muscle. "He was special, wasn't he? I think it was partly because he knew all along he was going to die, so he made every minute count. And he never wasted any time looking back and regretting things."

"Neither should we," Danny said.

Lightly cupping her chin, he raised her face to his. His eyes looked like pieces of blue cut right out of the sky. When he kissed her, a wave of heat flashed through her like lightning. He must have felt it too, she thought, because his arms tightened about her with sudden fierceness. He kissed her again, more deeply this time.

Alex became aware that she was half naked. Before, she'd only been thinking about how good the sun felt on her skin. Now, she thought how nice it was to feel Danny's hands travel over her bareness. She wasn't a bit self-conscious about it as she had been the last time they were together like this. It seemed right somehow. Natural. The way it was supposed to be.

They found a nest of dried pine needles under the trees and lay down. They took off the rest of their clothes and kissed a while longer. Then they just looked at each other without saying anything and she knew it was about to happen, what she'd been waiting for all this time.

Still, she hesitated. She lay against him for a minute or two, not moving—just savoring this special, private moment between them. Every detail carved itself into her memory. The dusty shafts of sunlight poking down among the branches, forming bright splashes on their bodies. The clean, sharp smell of the air, and the pleasant prickle of the pine needles underneath her. They crackled when she shifted her weight so that she was pressed up against the curve his body formed as he lay on his side, facing her.

"God . . . you're so beautiful," he whispered, pulling her in against him.

"So are you," she said. She smiled, reaching up to brush a stray needle from his hair.

After that, there was no need for words. They kissed some more. Danny stroked her side, then gently pushed her so that she rolled over onto her back. His lips moved over her neck, nibbling her shoulder, then tasting the hollow at the base of her throat. Alex felt as if the water rushing just beyond the trees were rushing through her, too—a current of warmth that flowed the way a river flows, sometimes quiet and deep, sometimes catching her up with a burst of sudden good feeling that left her breathless.

She didn't even mind when Danny got up for a minute to fumble in the pocket of his jeans.

"I didn't know we were going to . . . I mean, I put it in my wallet the night we went to my sister's and I just forgot to take it out."

Alex smiled. "I'm glad. You know, I wasn't thinking about *that*. It's a good thing you remembered . . . I mean, forgot. . . ." She could tell he was a little nervous from the way his hands trembled as he tore open the small foil packet. She realized he was probably embarrassed, because he'd never done this before, and he wasn't exactly sure how to go about it. "Hey look, nothing's ever easy the first time," she said.

He gave her a look that was halfway between a smile and a grimace. "It's not exactly the kind of thing you can practice at home."

They both laughed at that, and the moment of awkwardness dissolved. He lunged at her with a playful growl that dwindled to a murmur of contentment as he covered her body with his. He started kissing her again; this time his kisses seemed to reach right down into the deepest part of her. When they came together, she felt only a brief instant of pain, then the warm feelings took over again.

"I love you," he whispered in her ear.

She smiled. "I know."

"Oh, Alex . . . it feels so good . . . I . . . Oh!"

She didn't mind that it had ended so quickly. The warmth she'd felt lingered on as she lay huddled within the curve of his arm. She stared up at the sky through the branches. It was so incredibly blue . . . and so close, as if she could actually touch it if she reached up far enough. She felt that if she could do that, she would melt right into it and become a part of it, the way Noodle had.

Danny touched her cheek, bringing her back to earth. "Are you okay?"

"Mmm, it was nice." She grinned. "Definitely worth the wait."

"I was just thinking the same thing. I'm glad we waited. You were right about planning it out too much. Though it's probably a good thing we did that other time, otherwise . . . well, we wouldn't have been prepared this time."

A squirrel chittered in the branches overhead.

"Yeah, you're right. But I suppose it can't be like this every time."

"Why not? You'd look cute going around with pine needles in your hair."

She pretended to sock his shoulder. "You know what I meant."

"Yeah, I do. I was just teasing."

They lay there, smiling at each other.

Finally, she said, "We should probably start back. Everybody's going to wonder what happened to us."

"Yeah. You're right. We should."

Neither of them made a move to get up. Danny caught her earlobe between his teeth, biting gently.

"You're not making this any easier." She sighed.

"I wasn't trying to." He kissed her.

She looked at him in surprise. "Again?"

"Don't worry," he said. "We can't."

"Why not?"

"I, uh . . . well, the truth is, I only brought one of those things. I guess I wasn't thinking that far ahead."

"That's okay. I don't think either of us expected this day to turn out the way it did."

"Are you happy it did?"

She was quiet for a moment, sorting out the jumble of emotions she felt at this moment. Finally, she said quietly, "Yeah . . . I guess I am. The funny thing is, I don't feel guilty about it . . . about being happy, I mean. Somehow, I think Noodle would want me to be."

He brought his fingertip to her eyelid, catching the tear that trembled there before it fell. She read the question in his face.

"The sun was in my eyes," she told him.

He gave her a knowing look. "Yeah, I thought it must be something like that."

She felt a surge of gratitude toward him. Danny understood her. He really did. Maybe they weren't so different after all. Maybe, underneath it all, they really were meant for each other.

Alex scrambled to her feet and quickly got dressed. When Danny had finished putting on his clothes, she grabbed his hand and pressed it to her cheek, hard. Then she let go and skipped ahead of him down the trail.

"Come on," she said. "I'll race you to the bottom."

Chapter Thirteen

"Hand me the soap!" Elaine yelled. "Quick! He's getting me all wet!"

Alex dove for the shampoo bottle while Elaine, hose in hand, struggled vainly to keep Buster Brown, her big shaggy mongrel, from shaking water all over them. Elaine was giving him what she called his biannual bath out on the backyard lawn. Lori was trying to hang on to his tail. Kit had him by the collar. They made such a funny picture, Alex couldn't keep from laughing.

"I wish I had my camera," she said, lending Elaine a hand as she soaped his matted hide into a sudsy lather. "We could costar in the next Benji movie."

Elaine wrinkled her nose. "I don't think Benji ever smelled this bad. Phew! Wouldn't you know I have a date with Carl tonight? I just hope this stuff doesn't rub off. I'll go around smelling like dog all night." Her big glasses were flecked with soap. "Not exactly the ideal way to set a romantic mood."

Kit shot her a devilish grin. "I don't know. Some people have strange tastes. Maybe to some it's an aphrodisiac."

"Only to other dogs," Lori put in. She was wearing her blond hair scooped back in a ponytail. Her white pants were covered with mud streaks.

"I read once where this scientist did a study on how the smell of sweat stimulates the male sex drive," Kit argued. "They even came out with some kind of perfume made from sweat."

Alex giggled, directing the hose at Buster's wagging behind. "What did they call it—Eau de Locker Room?"

Elaine wrinkled her nose. "Just what I need. The way I sweat, I should have hordes of men chasing after me."

"What would you do with hordes?" Lori wanted to know. "Seems to me you're having enough of a problem with the one you've got."

"Has he kissed you yet?" Kit asked. She tried to duck as Buster let fly another shower of soapy droplets, but ended up getting splattered anyway.

Alex noticed the slow blush that was creeping up the sides of Elaine's neck. She hadn't told her friends about what had happened with Danny yet. She'd been waiting for the right time, but a week had passed since the

150

Senior Picnic, and she hadn't been able to bring herself to say anything yet. *Had something happened between Elaine and Carl, too*? she wondered.

Elaine had a dreamy look on her face in spite of how red it was. Kit must have seen it, too, for she shook a soapy fist at her in mock aggravation.

"He did! He kissed you—and you didn't tell us!"

"I was going to," Elaine said. "I was just waiting for the right moment."

"How did it happen?" Lori asked.

"It wasn't anything like I expected," Elaine said. "It was . . ."

"Start from the beginning," Kit interrupted. "I don't want to miss a single juicy detail."

Elaine hosed Buster off; then the four of them collapsed onto the overgrown grass, watching him charge off like a hairy cannonball, shaking himself furiously and zigzagging back and forth across the lawn. Alex laughed. She was thinking how good it was to be with her friends like this. Even a dumb little thing like washing a dog had turned out to be fun.

"Like I said," Elaine told them, "It wasn't the way I expected it to be. The way it happened was, Carl came over last night to help me baby-sit the twins when my parents went out. We were sitting on the couch after I finally wrestled them into bed, then he put his arm around me and . . . well, he kissed me."

"What's so unusual about that?" Alex asked, feeling somewhat let down.

"That's just the point." She sighed, taking off her glasses and wiping them on the tail of her navy-blue T-shirt. "After waiting all this time for him to work up to kissing me, I guess I was expecting something really dramatic. I had this fantasy of him sweeping me up the stairs to my room—like Scarlett O'Hara."

Lori seconded Elaine's sigh with one of her own. Alex knew that *Gone With the Wind* was Lori's favorite old movie. She'd seen it at least a dozen times. For a while, she'd even had a crush on Rhett Butler, although they'd pointed out he was old enough to be her father. Lori liked older men. Alex thought that was probably because it was safer to have a crush on someone much older, since most of the time nothing could come of it. Someone her own age Lori might actually get to like . . . maybe too much. Perry Kingston, for instance.

"The trouble with that scene," Kit said, "is that they don't show you what goes on *after* they get up the stairs. They skip over the best part."

Elaine fished a raggedy tennis ball from the overgrown bushes beside her, tossing it to Buster, who stopped dead in his tracks and just sniffed it curiously.

"He's supposed to be the kind of dog who

fetches things," she explained. "Only he never does. Once, I spent an entire summer trying to teach him. But one day, I accidentally threw a ball into our neighbor's yard and Buster went after it—only he came back with the steak Mr. Hennessey was barbequing instead. I stopped trying to teach him after that." She turned to look at her friends. "Do you think it's possible to be in love with someone if he's only kissed you once?"

"Sure it is," Kit said. "That's how I felt about Justin, although it took me a while to realize it. I guess I was just too scared of falling in love back in the beginning. I was afraid . . . oh, of everything bad that could happen if I did. I was right in some ways, too. I mean, there *are* some bad things mixed in with all the good things."

"Like thinking you might be pregnant?" Alex asked. She looked over at Kit, who sat Indian style on the grass, staring at the rusty old swing set Elaine's parents had never bothered to take down after the twins got too old to play on it.

Kit nodded. "I try not to think about it. I keep hoping the problem will just go away if I don't."

"Have you told Justin?" Lori asked.

"Yesterday. I had to. He wanted to know why I was going around crying all the time. He thought maybe I wanted to break up. So finally I just blurted it out. He said I shouldn't worry. That no matter how bad the situation was, we'd find a way to work it out together."

"I figured he'd say something like that," Elaine said. "He really loves you. People who love each other should stick by each other no matter what."

Alex found herself thinking about Danny, and how he'd helped her to get over the worst of her grief. She still wasn't sure how she felt about diving, but she *was* sure how she felt about Danny.

Kit turned to look at her. "What about you and Danny?" she asked. "Are you two getting back together again?"

It was on the tip of Alex's tongue to tell her friends about what had happened up in the woods that day of the Senior Picnic, but something stopped her at the last minute. *It was funny,* she thought. *She'd always been the one with the big mouth—ready to discuss what it would be like when she finally went all the way.* Now that she had, though, she'd found—the way Elaine had when Carl kissed her—that it wasn't anything like she'd expected.

What she'd experienced up on the mountain with Danny had been so . . . magical, was the only word she could think of to describe it. She was afraid that if she tried to tell them about it, some of the magic would rub off.

Someday, she would tell them. But not now. Not for a while.

"There's an intramural diving meet this coming Saturday," she said. "He wants me to come along and cheer for him."

"Aren't you competing in it?" Lori asked.

Alex shook her head. She wasn't sure if she could explain why to her friends. She wasn't even sure she understood it herself. All she knew was that the drive that had pushed her to win seemed to have gone out of her. Now that Noodle was gone, there just didn't seem to be any point in trying . . .

Fortunately, they didn't press her, and she was grateful for that. She was also grateful for the way they'd needled her into going to the picnic. She owed them a lot. *True friends*, she thought, *knew when to bug you as well as when to back off*.

Alex laughed as Buster picked the ball up and trotted over to Elaine, dropping it in her lap.

"I guess that goes to prove it's never to late to teach an old dog new tricks." Elaine picked it up gingerly. "Ugh! It's all slimy. Why'd you pick me, you dumb dog?"

Kit giggled. "He smells your dog scent, Elaine. He's attracted to you."

They all cracked up at that. Alex laughed so hard she nearly wet her pants. It felt good to laugh again with no holds barred. She thought about Noodle, and decided that, wherever he was, he was probably laughing right along with her.

"Nervous?" Alex asked Danny as they stood beside the diving board, looking out at the pool. He took off his sweatshirt and handed it to her. "Sure, I'm always nervous before I dive. Aren't you?"

Alex hesitated before admitting, "Yeah . . . I guess I was just too stubborn to admit it before."

She looked over at the bleachers. "Well, good luck," she said. "I saw you practicing a little while ago. You're really getting good."

"Not as good as you." Cupping his hand about her chin, he tipped her face up to meet his. Then, in front of everyone, he kissed her.

"What was that for?" she asked, pulling back with a little laugh, both pleased and embarrassed.

"That was a just-because-I-love-you kiss," he said, "Also, for luck."

"I thought I was supposed to kiss you for that."

He grinned. "Yeah, well, I figure it can work both ways."

When it was Danny's turn to dive, Alex went over and sat with the other members of her team, on a folding wooden chair. Coach Reeves came over and sat down next to her.

"I was sorry to hear about your brother, Alex," he began in that gruff, slightly gravelly voice of his. "I know how you feel. I lost a brother in Vietnam. It got me hard. If there's anything I can do, just let me know."

Alex opened her mouth to tell him she'd been thinking about quitting the team, but something stopped her. Maybe it was just the look in his eye when he talked about his brother. She decided she would tell him later. All she said was, "Thanks, Coach. I will."

She watched, shading her eyes against the sun that sparkled off the water like daggers, as Danny arched up in a nearly perfect swan dive. She felt her own body tensing. Afterwards, when he came up for air, she clapped until her hands hurt.

Coach Reeves spoke beside her. "You know what they say about falling off a horse, Alex. If you don't get right back up, you'll never ride again. Well, I figure it's the same with diving. That's why I entered you in this competition."

Alex whirled about in confusion. "What?"

"I can't say it was my idea. You can thank Danny for that." Seeing the look in her eyes, he added, "Once you get over being mad at him, that is." He brought out a tan canvas bag from under his chair. She recognized it instantly as hers. Somehow Danny had managed to sneak her swim togs out of her house.

"It's crazy!" she protested. "I can't dive now. I'm not prepared. I haven't practiced in over two weeks!"

Another voice broke in from behind. "You can do it." She turned to find Danny, dripping wet from the pool, staring at her with a determined expression. "It doesn't matter if you don't win. The important thing is just to get up there and try. I know you can do it, Alex."

"I'm scared," she confessed in a small voice.

Danny grinned. "Join the club."

Alex looked over at her coach in a panic.

"I used to throw up before every meet," he confessed sheepishly. "But don't let it get around. I wouldn't want it to ruin my tough-guy image."

Danny picked up her bag and handed it to her. "Looks like you're outnumbered."

Alex groaned, shaking her fist at him. "I'll get you for this someday."

A short while later, as she mounted the ladder to the diving board, Alex felt so nervous she was short of breath. Her heart banged against her rib cage. She didn't think she could go through with it. If she did, she would blow it for sure. All the determination that had once driven her was gone, leaving only stark, naked fear in its place.

When she reached the platform, she looked out over the packed bleachers, feeling the crowd's expectancy. Her palms started to sweat; even the soles of her feet were sweating. Oh, no, she couldn't do it! she would make a fool of herself!

Only the realization that she'd be making an even bigger fool of herself if she stepped down now propelled her forward. Automatically, she positioned herself for the reverse somersault her coach had slated her for. From where she stood, with her back to the crowd, all she could see was the pavement below where Danny stood, beaming up at her. He held up two fingers in the victory sign. His lips mouthed the words, *I love you*.

Suddenly, Alex stopped being so nervous. Sure, she wanted to do her best, but the warmth of Danny's smile and the special message that "I love you" had given her meant more than any judge's score.

She dove, arching backwards, feeling only the pure joy of stretching herself to the limit. She let the sky and water embrace her in a rush of blue, knowing that Danny would be waiting for her at the bottom.

**WHAT EVERY GIRL WANTS MOST OF ALL – TO BE PART
OF A COUPLE!**

BY LINDA A. COONEY AND M. E. COOPER

Meet the couples and couples-to-be at Kennedy High School in
this thrilling new series – pretty Chris and athletic Ted, popular
Phoebe and serious Brad, the dreamy Griffin and cool D.J. Peter,
plain Janie and vampy Lauri, sensitive Woody and troubled,
troublesome Brenda. Follow them through their first loves,
break-ups and crushes – the joys and pitfalls, the attractions and
the special moments.

One new title every month!

Available wherever Bantam paperbacks are sold.